Healing in the Ashes

Isabella Macejkovic

Contents

Chapter 1

She reminded me of a porcelain doll. The way her pale skin shined in the bright hospital lights. Her arms and legs, mere reminders of stick like figures. The bright blonde hair that everyone was jealous of was now gone, replaced by a grayish blonde wig that my mother insisted she buy her favorite daughter after the massive amounts of hair had begun to fall. "Water, Bails," she coughed.

Her bright blue eyes crept up from beneath her thick eyelashes and heavy lids, and they looked over in my direction. I hurriedly got up from that dreaded itchy chair in the room's corner and grabbed the tan pitcher from her bedside table. I poured her a cup and anxiously watched as her frail; toothpick like fingers lifted the plastic cup to her cracked lips. My eyes widened as her mouth turned up in a small smirk.

"Didn't we talk about the pity looks?" she joked, her voice small. She was losing energy quicker and quicker during that time. It's like one small movement of the hand, or stretch of the leg and she needed to rest again. I knew what this was doing to her. My question was though, did she? "I'm not pitying you," I sighed. My eyes dropped from hers and I moved a small piece of bright red hair from my view, making sure I didn't let her see my eyes. I could feel the water starting to gather at my lids and I didn't want her to see that I was giving up. "Hey," she said, sliding her hand over mine on the bedside. "You're supposed to be staying strong for me Bails. I need you through all of this remember?" I sniffed.

"I know, Lane. I know. I just..." "Stop it," she smiled. "I don't want this to turn into a sob fest over how much you're going to miss me, or how I look like pure crap right now. I want to remember us as happy sisters." I shook my head, the tears acting like glue, sticking my hair to my cheeks. I pushed them away and quickly wiped at the moisture. "You don't look like crap. You know you're gorgeous, Lanie. You always have been, even when you're lying in a hospital bed." "I know. Doesn't this lighting totally bring out my eye color?" she giggled.

I laughed along with her for a moment, cherishing it. I knew these were one of the last moments I was going to have with her. She was right. I didn't need to be bringing her down like this. I needed to stay strong for my older sister, and show her that either way; she was going to be alright, no matter where she ended up. "How can you be so happy when all of this," I gestured with my hands around the room and over her, "is going on?" She shook her head lightly. I noticed the small bruises forming beneath her eyes, and noted that they were getting darker since the last time I'd been here a mere two days ago. Lanie stroked my hand gently, comforting me without me asking to.

"Because I know what's going on. I'm accepting my fate now, Bails. I can't control what cards fate hands me, I just need to keep playing along until I can't anymore," she trailed off. I knew Lanie was trying to stay strong, and I was trying to stay strong for her, but this was all too much. Who's the asshole playing fate that decided to take my older and only sister away from me? She's my confidant, my go-to, my mood changer. I needed this girl in my life, and fate just up and decides to grant her with brain cancer. She never deserved to have this disease. Lanie's never done one wrong thing to someone in her life. She'd jump in front of a bus for a complete stranger if she could.

So why did "fate" think she deserved to die? "Stop doing that," she sighed, playfully. My eyes shot up to look at her face. "Doing what?""Over-thinking everything. You always make that face when you over-think. Your nose gets a little scrunched up and your eyes are wide open. You're not that hard to read you know," she smiled. "I'm not-""Bails, shut up, yes you are!" she giggled, tapping my hand lightly.

The doctors had told us a few days ago that Lanie only had a few days left. To say that we didn't take the news lightly was an understatement. Mom, I remembered, immediately threw herself against Dad, her tears staining his light colored button up shirt. Dad clutched her against his chest, keeping his head crooked in her neck. I curled up in my designated chair in the corner of the room and let the silent tears fall as I held my hand against my mouth, trying to stop the sobs from escaping my throat.

They told us that she would be able to fight this, that the odds were in her favor. Or, as Lanie put it, she was winning the game with her hand of cards life had dealt her. I looked over at her during that moment and she was...calm. Her body was lying straight, her eyes watching the doctor's every hand motion against his clipboard as he dragged the pen slowly through her chart, reading off her symptoms and how long they believed she had. She calmly nodded her head when he said she had a few days, and gave the doctor a small smile as he claimed how sorry he was for everything and bid his goodbyes.

I was shocked, to say the least. You're being told you're going to die in a few days time. Your newlywed husband is sitting at your bedside, clutching your hand for dear life, silent tears careening down his cheeks. Your parents are clutching onto each other like they can't bear to let go. And your younger sister is in a chair, praying to whatever god she can think of that you can fight this, and you're...smiling? It made no sense to me. But that was Lanie. She never made any sense. Lanie had her own opinions and ways of doing things that she thought were appropriate. It wasn't odd for a girl like Lanie to smile in the face of death, in the face of every loving family member who cried in front of her. She was the strongest girl I knew.

"Knock, knock," I heard Brayden's voice from the doorway across the room. "I'm not interrupting am I?" he asked, sheepishly. "No, you're okay Bray. I'll just leave you guys to it then," I sighed. As I went to get up, Lanie pulled me slightly and told me to come closer. "Bailey, anytime you need me, just look inside the box," she smiled. Her bright blue eyes had a sparkle to them for the first time in months. She looked just...happy. I smiled back at her, trying to keep the tears locked under my lids. I needed to be strong before I said goodbye. "I will." She intertwined our fingers together, holding on as tightly as she could. "I love you Bails, never forget that. I'll always be there if you need me, even if I'm not..." her voice was choked up, and I looked up into her eyes to see one stray tear fall.

She cursed quietly and wiped away the stray tear with her free hand. "See, you're making me cry! I didn't want to cry!" she laughed slightly. "Just...remember that, okay?" Why did our goodbye seem so final today? This wasn't like our usual goodbyes when I left the hospital for the night. Did she know what was going to happen? What wasn't she telling me? "Lanie don't make it seem so-" "Sh! Just remember that for me. I love you, alright?" My eyes welled up again and I nodded my head silently, hoping that this wasn't her last goodbye to me.

Hoping I would be able to come see her tomorrow and everything would be alright, and she would smile up at me like she did every day I came to see her. "I love you too, Lanie," I cried, squeezing her hand before she wrapped both of her frail arms around my body and pulled me in for a tight hug. I clutched onto her tiny frame, hoping it would work its magic and keep her here with me.

Then she laughed. She laughed. "Bray, I'm sorry. It's like we completely forgot you existed," she giggled. I picked myself up and looked over at Brayden, standing a little uncomfortably in the doorway, smirking. "It's okay, beautiful. I know you guys need that sisterly bonding time," he waved his hand carelessly. "I'm going to let you guys have your time. Love you, Lanie," I whispered. "To infinity and beyond, right?" she smiled, bringing up our childhood joke. "To infinity and beyond," I smiled, kissing her on the cheek and shuffling out of the doorway. I took one last glance back before heading completely out of the room and smiled as Brayden kissed Lanie full on the lips and she smiled brightly, looking as if she had finally won with her deal of cards.

And that was the last I saw of my beautiful, smiling sister. That blonde vision of vicarious optimism and glowing personality. And I'll always remember her as she told everyone she wanted to be remembered as. Being happy. After that day, I told myself I was going to strive to be what everyone envied of my sister. I was going to be strong and I was going to smile when everything seemed to go wrong. I would be optimistic and hope for the best in any situation I was placed in. I was going to be happy. Or at least that's what I thought. But life doesn't always go the way you want it to, does it?

Chapter 2

I was ten when I saw it. I was sitting cross-legged in front of the television screen, watching my favorite cartoons. As I giggled to something that had obviously been unbelievably funny to me at that age, I remember it being eerily quiet in my house. Mind you, it was never this quiet in my house, especially with my mother being almost eight months pregnant, and my dad always doing something handy around the house.

But that day, Dad got called in early. He came in my room while I was playing with my trucks and firmly noted that I had to clean my room. "No," I exclaimed, with the same amount of firmness. I didn't even make eye contact with him. I just went along playing with my cars again. "Excuse me?" he asked. "I don't wanna," I said, gliding my cars around the room. I heard his large footsteps intrude into my bedroom and saw his hand go to pick up one of my favorite trucks.

"Well until you feel the need to, you won't be seeing this," he exclaimed. I watched him walk away in horror as he took one of my favorite toys away from me. "I hate you!" I shouted as he walked out of my room. I silently sat on the floor and cried, hoping my mother would hear and somehow convince him to give me it back.

As the day wore on, it was mid morning and my Dad was nowhere to be found. I asked mom where he had gone and she explained how there was this big emergency and how he was just busy being a hero to all the little people again. When she told me this though, her grassy green eyes held some sort of worry that I couldn't quite pick up on. She pushed my black hair away from my eyes and told me to go watch cartoons for the morning, and wait for Dad to come home. That's how I ended up there, in front of the television in the quiet. A part of me was keeping an ear out for my mom, making sure she was okay. As I was getting into the good part of my show, my mom's friend Lynette came in and grabbed onto my hand. "Hey sweetie," she said, her tone a little too calm. "Want to come show me that new fire truck your father bought for you?" I always loved showing off my new fire truck.

My dad got it for me and told me that every time I worried for him when he went to work, that I could just look at that truck and know that he was safe from all harms, because all the firefighters protect each other, no matter what. "Sure," I smiled wide. I dragged her by the hand to my bedroom and picked up the shiny red truck and shoved it her way. But then I heard a shrill cry. I dropped the brand new truck onto the hardwood floor and it crashed into tiny blood red, metal pieces all over. I immediately ran to the living room and stopped still.

My mom was on her knees in front of the television, her face shiny from the fresh tears now pouring from her bright green eyes. I glanced towards the television, now noticing that my cartoons were no longer appearing on the big screen. Bright oranges and dusty grey brushes of colors were swirled around the television screen as a large building collapsed, floor by floor. My eyes widened at the sight, and I couldn't seem to take them away from the screen. "Gregory! Gregory!" My mother cried. She was still on her knees, her large belly covering most of her thighs, as she leaned forward, her palms pressing against her watery eyes. Lynette was by her side, rubbing her back soothingly, pushing pieces of her short black fringe away from her face.

Why was she screaming Daddy's name, I wondered? She said he was saving the people again, and that he would be home later. What did the building have to do with him? "Liz, come on sweetie. You need to get up, before you hurt the baby in that position," she said, using that same eerie tone she used with me, just moments before. She grabbed onto my mother's hand and pulled her up from the ground, while Mom sobbed loudly into her hands. "Mommy?" I questioned. I slowly walked over to her, grabbing her soaking wet hand. She finally looked up from the palms of her hands and something small flashed in her eyes, something I couldn't comprehend again.

Then she started sobbing some more, the sounds coming from her throat slowly breaking my heart, because I didn't know what I could do. I questioned Lynette the entire night. Why was grandma here? Why is Mommy still crying? What happened with that building? Was it just a movie she put on? And last, but surely not least, its night time, why hasn't Daddy come home yet? That night, on September 11, 2001, I lost my Dad to the fiery oranges and grey brushes of colors and smoke. All they kept saying was that he was a hero, that he tried helping some lady get out of the burning room. He should be honored for what he did, we shouldn't keep crying, they told us. I didn't care about all of that. Yes, he saved an innocent woman's life, but he lost his own. My Dad did not deserve to die. He deserved to come home, to be with his family, to keep saving more people, to do his job.

Who's the asshole acting as fate that allowed all of this crap to happen? Today's the anniversary of my Dad's death. We're all dressed in fancy clothes. My mom, dressed in a navy blue summer dress, with her hair pulled back. I'm dressed up in some fancy light blue button up, with black dress pants. And my brother, Greg Jr., is dressed in a dark blue polo with little khakis. As we stand in front of his grave, I'm running my hands through my messy, black hair, making it stand up everywhere. I can't stand to be near all of this sad, emotional bullshit anymore. I want to have my Dad come home. I feel little Greg pull on my hand, and look down. He's the spitting image of my Dad, with bright blonde hair and piercing baby blue eyes.

He's not sporting his usual toothy grin, but more a small frown, looking confused like he does every year that we come here."Evan," he says, still holding onto my large hand in his little one. "Can you tell me about Daddy again?" My mom looks up at me, giving me a small smile, her eyes clearly watery. She nods her head, giving her approval and looks back at Dad's site, fingering Dad's Medal of Honor in between her nimble fingers. "Well bud, Dad was a hero. He saved all these people from getting hurt," I explained. He smiled at me, seeming far less confused than he was before. "So he's kind of like Superman?" he smiled, sporting that same toothy grin that I knew so well. I smiled back, gripping his little hand in mine. "Yeah, kind of like Superman." "Cool," he noted, looking back at his grave site.

"Do I look like Daddy?""Exactly like him bud," I nodded, fingering his skinny, silver dogs tags that I had placed around my neck.

"You're definitely just like Dad," I murmured. "Alright, I think we're ready to go," my mother sighed, looking up at me. "You ready, sweetie?" "I uh, think I need a minute," I told her, nodding my head towards his site to show her I wanted time alone with him. "Let's go, Greg. You're brother will be there in a minute," she said softly, grabbing onto his hand and leading him towards the car. As I watched them walk away, I turned my back towards them and sighed heavily.

I felt like these bricks were lying on my chest, keeping my breathing at a rapid, unsteady pace. There was so much weight shoved on my body that I felt as though I couldn't function normally anymore.

"Dad," I breathed. "You see how big he's gotten? He's the spitting image of you, no matter how big he gets," I smiled a little to myself. "We have this talk every year and I feel like it never gets me anywhere. Because the sole fact of it is, I just want you back, Dad. And I'm so, so sorry. For everything that happened that morning. I don't hate you. I need you back. Mom doesn't even want to replace you yet, and it's been eleven years. Hell, I don't think she can find another guy like you. She needs you Dad. We all need you.

I just wish you could be back here with the three of us again," I breathed, fingering the tags in my hands, turning them left and right. I felt as though if I held onto them long enough, it would bring me closer to him somehow, in some mysterious way. I felt a small amount of moisture prick at my lids and quickly coughed, rubbing my eyes fervently with my fists. I kissed my hand and placed it on his gravesite. "I love you, Superman," I said, before I walked away. I made my way back to my mom's car, gripping onto the metal of the tags roughly, silently wishing he could just come back so I could say sorry the right way.

Chapter 3

" Sweetie, you need to get the hell out of bed," my Dad laughed at me. I slid the dark blue covers on Lanie's bed over my face and sunk further into the bed, trying to hide from him.

"Bailey Renee, you need to get up and help me plan this thing. We talked about this..." he urged. I felt a firm hand grip at the tops of the covers, trying to pull them off of my face. It was Saturday morning in late September and I was still sleeping in Lanie's bed, even though it's been two years since she's passed. I liked to think that if I slept in her room every night that it somehow brought me closer to her, in a way that I couldn't quite explain to anyone else.

At first I started lying here every night because it smelled like her, and I missed her so much that just the smell of her left on her dark blue pillow case could be satisfactory enough for me to get a good night's sleep. Now, I can't even imagine moving back into my own room at this point. "Dad, can't you plan the benefit without me?" I groaned, pulling the covers with me as I turned onto my right side, away from his heaping presence. He laughed that hearty, country laugh that I was so used to hearing.

"Bails, I asked for your help because your mother isn't exactly around much, what with her firm heating up at the moment." "I told you to stop calling me Bails," I murmured. "You know that

Lanie used to-" He stiffened for a second, and sighed. "I'm sorry. I didn't mean to do that. You know I just got used to calling you-" "I get it, Dad," I whispered. I pulled the covers down a little under my eyes and looked up at him. His face held pure sorrow as his chocolate brown eyes started to water up. Even after two years of this emotional rollercoaster, the mere mention of Lanie's name was enough to start up a whole batch of crying fests. Every time each one of us talked to each other in this house, it was like we had to tip-toe over certain subjects that would bring up the memory of her.

Like, I couldn't talk about going to a bakery in the mornings without Mom starting to crumble, because that was Lanie's old job. Even the slightest hint to a ham sandwich and it was like the whole house would fall apart, because that was her favorite food.

I sighed heavily and held onto my Dad's hand. His eyes grew wide and he looked down at me through my reddish strands of hair in my face. "I'll be down in your office in twenty minutes, okay?" He smiled small and used his other hand to push the pieces of red out of my eyes, kissing my forehead. "Thanks a bunch kiddo." I gave him a small smile as he proceeded to my open doorway and waited for him to shut the door before I turned back around to face my wall, the dark blue covers snuggled up under my chin.

I felt a small tear fall down my cheek and caught it immediately with my hand. I sniffed, trying to hold back the breakdown that I knew was about to come. I was tired of being upset. I was tired of crying and pretending everything was okay. It's been two years; you figure I would be over this by now.

I hadn't even truly sat down with my parents and talked about how I felt. It was as though when Lanie died that I suddenly became invisible to everyone in my family. I always knew Lanie was the favorite, and I never tried to change that, because I knew I couldn't possibly take her place. I didn't want to take her place. Who could possibly take that blonde vision's place in this world? She was one of kind. The only reason my Dad was making such a big deal over me getting out of bed before ten on a Saturday morning was because Mom was out on another case for her newly opened law firm, and I was the only one around to help him with this benefit concert he was planning for the Ladder 24 firemen.

You see, my father's this big wig in the country music world. The name Phillip Keys is a name that any member in the country music business could tell you about. He was friendly with everyone, had already won 3 grammys in his short two year career, and has sold out shows from here in New York City, all the way to Japan. And the Ladder 24 house has been a house that he'd always called home.

His father was a firefighter for 40 years before retiring at the age of 65. My Dad practically grew up in that house from the time he was two, and it's always been a place that he's held close to his heart. With it being almost a week since the anniversary of the tragic 9-11 event, my Dad wanted to give back to the men who had lost their friends to the dusty smoke and blazing fires, and salute those who had lost their lives in general. Phil felt that giving back with his music was the best thing he could do. And last, but surely not least, he was giving all of his concert proceeds back to the men who he had called family since before he could remember.

I'm sitting in Lanie's bed, awestruck that my father, the man who had given birth to me and called me his flesh and blood, was more sentimental to a bunch of firemen that he barely knew, than he was to me. My Dad should have let me cry on his shoulder when we heard the news of Lanie's passing. He should have held my hand at the funeral as we all crowded in the graveyard in a black cluster of shirts and ties, instead of just hugging my mother.

He has another daughter left on this earth, so why did it seem like as soon as Lanie died, he'd had no responsibilities left to take care of anymore?

About an hour later I'd made my way downstairs to my father's office. I had slipped on a pair of black leggings and a light green, slightly stretched out shirt that hung past my shoulders. My feet grazed against the plush, white carpet as I quietly padded through the house. I tousled the light red waves away from my eyes and let out a deep breath that I didn't know I had been holding. I slowly turned the golden knob and knocked slightly before opening the door all the way. "You can come in," he called to me. I closed the large wooden door behind me, and my feet turned cold as they met the hardwood floors of my Dad's office. It was strikingly cold I noticed as I folded my arms against my chest, feeling small goose bumps make their way against my skin.

"Come sit," he said, urging me with his hand to take the small leather chair next to him. He was lounging in his larger, black leather computer chair, his dark brown eyes focused on something on his large silver laptop. "Ah, this venue is perfect!" "What venue?" I asked, talking quietly. I still never really felt quite comfortable in ordinary conversations with my Dad, considering they only happened about once a week. "This new retro theatre that Lina just emailed me about," he smiled, clicking fiercely through all of the pictures on the theatre's website that his assistant had sent him. "Seems really cool, Dad," I smiled slightly, faking interest.

"You bet it does!" he laughed, already tapping the theatre's number into his iPhone's screen. I rested my back against the small chair, and pulled his leather bound planning notebook from his large desk and started making a list for him so he wouldn't forget to do anything. That's all he really needed from me anyway. As I finished with the last words being, "Call Kyle, your guitar manager, and make sure he has your guitars dropped off at the place the morning of," I pushed the book back into a spot I knew he would remember to look at it, and stood up.

"Hang on one second," he said to the manager of the venue on the phone. He covered the mouth piece with his large hand and looked up at me with concern. The concern, I noted, mostly for himself because he thought I'd decided against helping him.

"Where are you going?" he asked, anxiously. "It's all right there in your book, Dad. Everything you need to remember to do. Just check off everything as you go," I shrugged. Not like you need me for anything else, I said to myself. He smiled slightly as first, and then frowned for a quick moment. He seemed to be thinking quickly as to what to say, other than a small thank you, which would have been enough for me. After a few more seconds, he smiled again, reaching into his back pocket. As he pulled out his wallet, he set his iPhone down and pulled out two crisp one hundred dollar bills, the small corners slightly bent from the wear of its home.

"Buy yourself something nice for the benefit, then?" he said, smiling widely at me, handing me the bills.

Was he serious? He was thanking me by giving me money? Were a 'thank you' and an 'I love you' just too hard to suffice? "Thanks Dad," I said, a tight lipped smile making its way onto my face. It's nice to know that I helped with everything and I don't even get a thank you, just a token of affection with two hundred dollars. He picked his iPhone back up and started talking animatedly, waving his hands around like a mad man, excitement clear as day on his unshaven face. I trudged back up to the room I was in an hour ago, and slipped back into the familiar confinements of the bed. I wrapped the covers around me like a cocoon and pressed my eyes closed forcefully, silently hoping that I could stop the tears that I knew were about to fall. Not that anyone in this house would notice anyway.

Chapter 4

W hy is it this warm in the first week of October; I thought as I slipped on a pair of loose fitting, dark washed skinny jeans and white button up. I rolled the sleeves up to my elbows and quickly fixed my mess of black heap on the top of my head. I pushed it back a bit, so it stood up slightly on the top of my head. It was too warm to be messing around with gel and other products that I knew would melt under the burning rays otherwise.

It was the beginning of October in New York, and it was almost eighty-five degrees. By now, the clouds should be covering the sky in grey smog and colder air should be forming. It shouldn't be sweltering and sticky outside right now. I shook my hair out a little more and made my way downstairs. I kissed my mother on the top of head as she played with a frying pain filled with pancake batter. "Pancakes today?" I asked, smiling down at her small, five foot frame. She smiled up at me beneath her dark eyelashes and winked.

"Just for my boys," she grinned. "Speaking of that, where's baby Greg?" "Mom! I'm not a baby anymore! I'm ten years old for Pete's Sake," my baby brother's voice protruded through the kitchen opening as he looked up at my mother with a pitying look. "Well sweetie, when you're almost twenty-one like Evan, than maybe I'll think about not calling you baby anymore," she said, kissing him on the forehead, pushing his blonde hair back from his eyes. I laughed at him as he held the same frown when he sat down at the table in front of me.

"Shut up, Evan!" He said, sticking his small tongue out at me. I stuck mine out back out at him, and tapped him on the side of the head. "Oh Jesus, you'd think that after he passes the legal age of adulthood that he'd stop sticking his tongue out at others," my mother sighed, placing a paper plate filled with mouth-watering pancakes in front of me. I immediately dug in, laughing at her comment as I chewed. "Ah, I forgot to tell you, sweetie. The 24 boys called the other day and they wanted to invite us to the benefit concert that Phillip Keys is holding next Friday! Oh, that man has such a voice, and such a cute-"

"Mom!" I yelled, cutting her off from gushing about the old man any further. I wasn't much into country music so I didn't understand why she was telling me all of this. She smiled sweetly at me. "But you'll go right?" "No offense to the Ladder 24's, Mom, but why would I want to go to a country event when I don't even like country music?" I asked, shoveling the last piece of pancake into my mouth, immediately wiping my mouth with a napkin. "Because it would mean a lot to your father..." she murmured, clearly trying not to bring him up in front of Greg Jr. With the mention of my father's name, Greg Jr. would either cry instantly, wishing he got the chance to meet him, or be excited and want to know more about him. It was a pretty sore subject in my house when it came to little Greg, but wasn't that hard for my Mom and I to speak of when we were alone.

"Daddy would like it?" he questioned, his voice rising. He looked up at Mom with those large blue eyes filled with excitement. When he was happy at the mention of Greg Sr., he was always trying to find ways he knew would please him. It was like Greg's little way of showing appreciation for the man who he never had the chance to know. It was his way of being closer to him without him actually being there.

"He would," she said, slowly and cautiously, trying to gauge his reaction. My Mom and I say silently on the edge of our seats, the large majority of us expecting a massive outburst in five seconds. "Oh my god, Evan! Can we go, can we go? I want to be there for Daddy. Please!" he bounced up down on the wooden dining chair and looked at me expectantly.

A small part of me really did want to do this for Dad, too, even if I didn't like this Phillip Keys guy. I kept eye contact with little Greg as I slowly nodded my head in agreement. His large blue eyes immediately lit up and he ran to hug me quickly. "Thank you, thank you, thank you, Evan! Now I need to go pick out a good outfit for Daddy!" he said, rushing out of the room, leaving his uneaten breakfast behind him. I gripped the dog tags lightly, out of habit. "You're a sweet man, Evan," she said, lightly. She kissed my head and looked me straight in the eyes, her green ones serious.

"Your father would be very proud of you for doing this for baby Greg," she said. I just nodded my head slowly and picked up my plate, placing in the trashcan. I didn't know how I was going to deal with this. Yes, the Ladder 24 guys have been a huge help for the past ten years since Dad passed away, but anything involving my Dad was always a sore subject. I couldn't deal with this alone. Mom would be there, but she'd be too googly-eyed for that Phillip guy, and little Greg would be busy with the rest of the guys. I held onto the silver tags and repeated that I could do this, over and over in my head.

I could do this. After I made it to my car for a bit of fresh air, I called Aaron. Aaron Meehan was the pure definition of a best friend. If you needed a place to stay, his couch was open. If you needed money, he'd have his wallet in hand in thirty seconds. And if you needed a life to be saved, he'd be the one showing up in the yellow and red suit with fire equipment in hand. He was a firefighter, just like my Dad had been. And he's working for the Ladder 24 men as well. My Dad even knew Aaron as a kid before he passed away. Aaron's only about three years older than me, and we shared the same block name before he moved away with his mother when I was 15.

We grew up together and our families were inseparable. I knew I could always count on him to make things better, especially when it came to things going on with my Dad. "Hey, what's up Ev?" he exclaimed, clearly excited to hear from me. "Hey dude. Nothing really, just driving around is all..." I let my voice fall out. The thoughts of that stupid day back in '01 when everything in my life crumbled scratching at the surface. "Ah, so you're thinking again?" I shook my head, forgetting that he wasn't next to me. He knew me too well. "You know me. I just...Mom told me you guys were holding some benefit thing?"

"Yup," he said, popping the 'p'. "Phil Keys is holding it for us. Cause you know Chief Keys was his Dad and all. He always feels like he needs to give back to us. Which I don't think he does..." "I don't care about the whole country dude. This is my Dad's home we're talking about here, Aaron. His friends. This was his life for as long as I can remember. Now I have to go back and relive all that shit again? I don't think I can do it..." I sighed, gripping the steering wheel with my one hand a little tighter. As the conversation turned serious, I pulled over, into a grocery store parking lot, with the air conditioner on blast.

"Evan, man, you have to stop this. He died almost ten years ago. You can't do anything about what you said that day, you know that. Some of his best friends are in this Ladder, and they would love to see you. They see Jr all the damn time. It's time you step up and talk to all of them again. You can't avoid all of this for the rest of your life." I felt that stupid brick on my chest feeling creep up on me again for what felt like the thousandth time since Dad had died. I clawed at my chest, stretching out the fabric of my white button up. Why had I even worn this damn thing in this heat? "I can hear you freaking out through the phone man. Calm down. Breathe," Aaron whispered through the phone. He was probably at work and didn't want the other guys to hear what was going on. But, I steadied my breathing none the less, and sighed again.

"You're right, man. I know I need to fix this shit. It's not good for me, or for anyone I've been avoiding. How are the guys anyway?" "They're doing pretty good. They're all excited to be kid-free and drunk off their asses next week," he laughed. "I bet they are," I laughed. I ran my hand through my hair again, and thought of Little Greg and what this would do to him if I decided not to go. I picked up the tags off of my chest and stroked them gently with my fingers. "I'm going to do it, Aaron." "Good," he exclaimed. "I knew you would. You just need to get out of your own head for a while. This will do you some good dude. Plus, I heard Phil Keys daughter is pretty hot," he laughed again. I laughed with him and kept the smile on my face all the way back to my house. I think all I needed was a little reassurance from someone other than my own mother, to know that I could move on and deal with all this finally. It's been long enough, like Aaron said. I could do this.

Chapter 5

" I just want to thank Phil for making all of this possible. And for helping us raise $5,000 for the Ladder 24 men! Cheers!" I sat on the side of the stage, watching this man named Ed. He was the current chief of the station, wearing a too-tight black t-shirt with matching black jeans and large boots. His faded blonde hair was ruffled and flat against his wrinkling head. He raised his bottle of beer to the crowd ahead of him, and took a sip. The whole room cheered and called Phil back for more entertainment.

The night turned out very well in my Dad's favor. Hundreds of people had bought tickets and filled up the small theatre. It reeked of beer, sweat and cigarette smoke as firemen laughed and belted out drunken lyrics to my Dad's songs, hanging off of their wives arms. Some wore cowboy hats and pretended they were Phil Keys for a day, faking a terrible country accent while they sang. I shook my head at them, leaning against an amp case on the side stage, sipping from my water bottle.

The lights dimmed once again, everything going pitch black, as my Dad walked right past me and onto the stage, his pale wooden acoustic guitar hanging off of his right arm. His face had lit up at the calls of his name and the claps of appreciation, as he began with a single strum. He started the verse of his most popular song;

"Big Blue Eyes" and the room became ecstatic with cheering and men belting out the beginning words.

"Big Blue Eyes" was written about my older sister, Lanie, of course. He wrote it for her the week after she passed away. That was how my Dad dealt with emotions; he sat down in his office, picked up that acoustic, and blended the music with the mess in his head. I believe this was why he was so popular in his form of music. People could honestly and full-heartedly relate to the lyrics Phil came up with. It was a way for my Dad to get away, and for every else to as well.

As I watched Phil on stage, I noticed him look up as he sang. He looked past the blinding stage lights, past the black bars holding the equipment, past the dark red bricks creating the ceiling. He was singing to Lanie. He was showing her that this was about her, that he would love her for the rest of his life and beyond. Phil was connecting with his favorite daughter as though no one was in the crowd, as if it was just him and Lanie in the room, all to themselves.

I felt a slight pang in my heart as I realized again that Lanie was never coming back. But the pang, I noted, was also because deep down I knew...I knew that I would never have a connection like that with my father. I knew Lanie was his favorite and he wishes with every fiber in his being that he could bring her back to him. He doesn't want the daughter that he has left; he wants the one that he lost, because no one could replace Lanie Keys. Not even her younger and almost alike sister.

I wiped a lone tear from beneath my eyelid, not wanting to mess up the massive amounts of makeup I had shadowed onto my lid, and took a deep breath. I placed my water bottle onto the amp case and walked further backstage, looking for a way out. I felt my chest heavily rising and falling, as though I couldn't get the weight off of it. My breathing was rapid and my heart was running a mile a minute. I felt the known panic attack coming and I needed to find fresh air quick.

Running away from the many stage workers around me, I landed in front of a door labeled "ROOF" in white, thick paint. I slammed the big black door open and ran up the stairs towards my destination as fast as my high-heeled sparkly gold shoes could carry me. I made it to the top, flinching when the large metal door slammed shut behind me. My hand clutched at my chest, hopelessly trying to calm my breathing and rapid heartbeat.

The beginning of fall had made the night a little windy and much cooler than a hot summer day, and I felt my reddish curls blow behind me, away from my face. I felt like I couldn't remove the bricks constricting my chest, and I wanted to desperately make it stop. I took long, deep breaths and rapidly wiped the wet drops off my cheeks. My other hand was clutching the edge of the roof's siding, as I bent over, regaining my composure. Then I heard a noise behind me, like a person clearing their throat. As my heartbeats calmed down and my breathing became normal, I slowly turned my head to the noise.

My eyes widened at the sight of a guy perched on the far side of the roof's edge. He was sporting dark, messy midnight black hair that pushed up a little at the front of his face, without the help of hair product. From the shading of the bright streetlights I noticed his eyes were a light green, as they shone from beneath the lights. He was skinny, but muscular with his toned arms peeking from the lengths of his white, button-up collared shirt. The shirt was loosely tucked into a pair of loose fitting skinny black jeans, which ended beneath a pair of black converses. "I didn't know someone was-""No, it's okay. I didn't want to…interrupt you. I figured I would let you calm down first." His voice was rough, but smooth all at the same time, if that was even possible. He pushed up one of the sleeves of his shirt, his other hand holding a rusty brown bottle of beer. He sipped a little from it, still keeping his eyes on me. "But, are you alright?" he questioned. It was strange to me how a boy whose name I didn't even know asked me questions with such sincerity that my own parents hadn't even used before.

I nodded my head lightly, my light red curls bouncing along my shoulders. My choice of a white summer dress and black stockings didn't seem like such a good idea at the moment, because the cold fall night was seeping into my skin and I started to shiver a little. But at that moment, I didn't know if the shiver was from the cold, or from the boy perched in front of me. "Good," he nodded, taking another sip from his drink. He had to have been older than me, I noted, if he had gotten his hands on alcohol. The theatre's bar was ID only and very strict on whom they served to. That, or he was severely sneaky.

"I'm sorry. You probably wanted to be alone up here. I should go," I said hurriedly. I started to quickly walk back to the big metal door and pulled at the old, golden knob. The door didn't budge. I was locked up here. With a boy I didn't know. In a summer dress, freezing my ass off. Oh hell. "Locked out?" he asked, grinning beneath his bottle. I blushed, and nodded, pushing my bangs out of my eyes. I suddenly became very interested in my fresh manicure, trying with great difficulty not to look up at him, trying to conceal my embarrassment.

"I was too. Well I guess I still am now. That's why I'm up here. I came up here for fresh air, and ended up having to stay here, with no way out," he shrugged. He used a big hand to push some more of that messy lush of hair from his face. "I'm guessing you needed fresh air too?" he inquired, raising a dark eyebrow. I only nodded in agreement, not sure where my voice had gone. The fact that this boy, a total stranger, had seen me at my worst at first glance was enough embarrassment for one night. I didn't even know what kind of trouble my mouth could get me into if I spoke. "Can you talk?" he laughed.

I went to nod my head again, but decided against it. He noticed my stupid action and chuckled again, throwing back another swig of his beer. Either he was boarder-line tipsy or I really was embarrassing the hell out of myself. "I'm sorry. People don't usually see me like," I paused. "Like well that," I said, pointing to the side of the roof where my previous meltdown had been. "No worries. Trust me; I know how that," he pointed where I had, "feels. You want a drink?" He picked up another rusty brown colored bottle off of the ground that was next to about three other bottles and held it in my direction. One of the bottles was already empty next to him, and the second hadn't been touched yet. I watched the closed bottle closely as I contemplated taking it for a second, knowing how odd it was to obtain a drink off of a stranger.

"Don't worry. I wouldn't drug you," he smirked, shaking his head at me like he could read my mind. I nodded my head as he popped the top off for me and handed it back to me. I know how idiotic I must have been in that moment, excepting a drink from someone I didn't know but it was closed with the top still on, and I really needed a somewhat escape from the catastrophe downstairs. I pushed it towards my lips and took a big sip. I wasn't a stranger to drinking, considering Lanie and I would drink together in her room most times when our parents were away. And our parents were away a lot. He smiled at my actions, noticing I wasn't being lady like and taking baby sips from the bottle. After drinking almost half of the bottle in safe silence with this new boy, I looked up at him.

"Why did you need fresh air?" I blurted, suddenly curious about the guy before me. "God," he threw his head back, looking up at the glowing stars above us. "Do you know how long of a story that is?" he asked, looking back at me again. I walked a little closer, sitting down many inches away from him on the side of the roof. "No, I wouldn't know. I don't even know who you are." I didn't understand where my random bout of courage had come from. I usually didn't open up well with others that I didn't know. This was definitely a first. "I'm a guy you probably wouldn't care to know about," he smirked, like this was a good thing that he thought so low of himself. After taking another sip of beer, he looked in front of him; staring at something I couldn't grasp in the dark night.

"And why is that?" I asked, playing with a curl, twirling it around my finger. "You see, I'm not a nice guy," he said, shaking his head. He pushed more hair back again, sighing. "Still not understanding why..." I prodded, wanting to know more. "Let's just leave it at that," he murmured. Following his statement came another few moments of silence until he looked up at me again. "What about you? Why did you need the fresh air?" his grassy colored eyes were suddenly upon my own and I felt like I was under inspection. I cleared my throat. "Um...you see, my Dad's kind of the guy who's playing right now. It's a long story, but I needed a break...from all of...that," I gestured towards the door.

His eyes widened a little. "No way! Your Phil Keys' daughter? My Mom's like in love with that dude..." he shook his head, laughing lightly. At the mere mention of his Mom his whole face lit up instantly, the grassy colored orbs shining. I nodded my head. "I'm guessing you're a firefighter?" He stiffened a little, his hand clutching the bottle tighter. That glowing face disappeared suddenly and was replaced with a wall; a wall to certainly keep me back out. "No," he said, clearing his throat. "A firefighter's son, then?" I prodded further.

His body didn't move, as he still remained stiff. "Mhm," he nodded, not going into any sort of detail. He chugged another sip from his bottle. "I'm sorry. I just...noticed your tags," I said, pointing to his neck. I embarrassed myself more, like I knew I would have. He probably wouldn't want anything to do with me anymore because I was such a sorry excuse for a conversationalist. "It's alright. You were curious." The man in front of me gulped another large amount of alcohol from the rusty bottle and placed the empty remainder of it down onto the siding. He played with the rim, running his long finger around the opening again and again, looking as though he was contemplating something hard.

"I'm sorry. I really didn't mean-" "What about you? What's with the tattoo?" he asked, cutting off my apology and pointing to my wrist. He was referring to the solid black, infinity symbol etched on my wrist, with the words "and beyond" intersecting between a line on the symbol. It was my turn to put up a front this time, and I swallowed almost noticeably. I pulled my arm back so it was resting against my lap, away from his sight. "It's nothing. Just some silly tattoo," I lied blatantly. He already saw me break down. I wasn't about to let some strange boy into my personal life even more.

I studied him as the safe, oddly comforting silence came upon us again. He had a strong jaw line and slightly full lips. He had dark eyelashes surrounding the grassy colored eyes and almost flawless skin. It was strange to me how a boy who seemed so perfect could look so sad. "I'm Evan, by the way," he noted suddenly, glancing up at me, then back down to the bottle again. "Bailey," I whispered, interested in his motions and what his thoughts were running to. His phone went off then, making a small chirp. He picked it out of the back pocket of his skinny jeans and smiled small. "My little brother," he smiled. "He gets his first phone and he's suddenly worried about every place I've gone too. I'm going to see if he can come unlock the door for us," he said to me as he tapped away in reply on his touch screen.

As he placed the phone back in his pocket, I watched him closely. There was something about this guy, something I couldn't quite grasp onto yet. I suddenly became so interested in what he was about, what he was thinking, what made this gorgeous boy so sad. "If Phil's your Dad, is that girl he talks about in that song my Mom always sings...your sister? I mean it's obviously not about his wife. It has to be about his daughter." "How do you know it's not about me?" I asked, raising a thin eyebrow.

"Because your eyes aren't baby blue," he deadpanned. "They're hazel," he looked up at me with his own grassy green eyes, not letting me let go of the eye contact. I felt goose bumps rise on my arms as the wind blew around us. This time, I knew the bumps weren't from the cold. Moments later I jumped as I heard a voice. "Evan!" came a child's voice from the direction of the door. He was only around three and a half to four feet tall. He had light blonde hair, spiked up just like his said brother's and baby blue eyes to match. The image of my smiling sister came to mind as he held open the door, smiling widely at the man before me.

"Hey bud," he grinned widely. This was the first time I've seen him smile like that in the thirty minutes I'd been up here with him. He quickly walked over to the boy, picking him up and holding him on his side. I smiled at the cute image before me. He looked over at me, gesturing for me to come over. "Don't want you locked up here again. You coming, Bailey?" he asked. I nodded, setting my bottle down next to his that he had left on the roof's siding, clicking slowly over to the boys in my high heels.

As we made our way downstairs, we departed without goodbyes as the little boy pulled Evan over in the opposite direction. I was about to mumble a goodbye of some sort when I ran straight into my mother, looking highly displeased. "Bailey, where have you been?" she asked, her voice raising a few octaves as she spoke. "I needed a bit of fresh air," I mumbled over the loud bass thumping from my Dad's still ongoing show. "Your father needed you to help the guitar tech. You're the only who could help him. God knows I know nothing about those damned instruments," she said, shaking her blonde bob of hair back and forth. Even at a concert, she was dressed like an uptight lawyer.

She was sporting her usual black pants suit and clicking witch heels. "I'm sorry, I'll go help him now," I said, moving around her to the graying guitar tech on the side stage. She grabbed my arm with her skinny, tan fingers and pulled me back. "It's too late for all of that," she hissed. "The Warren's are making a speech for one of the firefighters. Your father's basically done after this song." "Sorry, Mom," I mumbled, looking down at the shiny wooden floors beneath my feet. She waved her hand and made her way to the dressing room in the back, away from all of the noise that she clearly hated. I sighed, throwing my hair behind me and walking over to the side stage, watching my Dad finish his last song, strumming the final chords. Everyone clapped and screamed loudly for him, but he shushed them all into the microphone to get their attention.

"Thank yall so much for all the support!" he drawled with his heavy country accent. "Now here are the Warren's. Give it up!" he said, raising his arms for the theatre to make noise for the said family. My Dad patted my shoulder with his free hand as he walked past me, and straight to my Mom in the dressing room. I stayed put, not wanting to be near either of them. I waited for the Warren's to take the stage and my eyes widened at the sight before me. The man from the roof and his blonde little brother came forward, along with a woman with short, dark hair like her older son's.

"You know Greg loves all of you guys!" the woman said into the microphone. "Thanks so much for raising all of this money for his Ladder 24 foundation boys!" "I love you Daddy!" the little boy yelled into the microphone from Evan's side, looking up at the ceiling like my Dad had before when singing for Lanie. Evan just smiled, his eyes scanning over all of the men hooting and cheering for the family. But from a close glance you could tell there was a trace of sadness hidden beneath his features. Where was this supposed Greg Warren? What am I missing?

Chapter 6

I smiled at all the men cheering for my Dad's name politely, like a good person should. But, deep down I wanted to scream at the top of my lungs off of rooftops that this wasn't right. He deserved to live a full life with his beloved wife, with his two sons, and to see them live a fulfilling life. Who could take someone's life away when they've barely started living it; when they were a hero to so many people? The only time my smile even reached my eyes was when I saw Aaron in the back, dressed in a dark green t-shirt and dark washed jeans, hooting with his hands around his mouth, "Yeah Greg!" He nodded his head with a smile on his face at only me, showing me his approval at my decision to stick out the concert for my family, for my Dad.

"Daddy's definitely Superman right, Evan? Cause everyone loved Superman?" he asked me, looking up at me with those big blue eyes that I could sincerely never say no to, no matter the circumstances. I smiled small at him. "Yeah buddy. Everyone loves Dad." He grinned in approval at me and grabbed onto my hand with his smaller one, clutching tightly. The pressure from the hand squeeze felt like the pressure going on in my chest. My heart clenched at the hoots of my Dad's name, knowing he couldn't physically be here to see that so many people loved him, just like I did.

To see that everyone raised $5,000 for his foundation that Mom had put in his name. When a room full of men, some friends, some family, most even strangers who've only heard about him in random conversation, come together to create such a thing for one man, you know that you've touched many people's lives in that moment.

Running my eyes over the crowd, they managed to land side-stage to the girl that I'd met on the rooftop just a mere few minutes before. She was looking directly at me with a mixture of confusion and deep thought plastered on her face. When she noticed me staring back at her, her big hazel eyes widened for a moment and then fell to the floor, her pale cheeks tinting into a shade of baby pink. I smiled a little, liking that she did that. I had no idea why I liked that, considering the only thing I really knew about her was that she had the same breakdowns that I had and that her name was Bailey.

When I tried to pressure her into more questions whilst we drank our beers together, it was like an immediate wall had gone up and she barricaded me out from anything too personal. I mean, I'm not one to talk because as soon as she mentioned me being a firefighter's son, I went ramrod straight and threw that same wall of protection up from her as well. But hey, when your father dies I believe you're allowed to have a little bit of emotional protection for your heart right? God only knows what was wrong with this girl. She seemed as fucked up as I was, emotionally speaking. Just because we had the same breakdowns doesn't mean I had to let this strange girl know anything pertaining to me. If I had been a little more drunk, I probably would have spilled everything willingly.

Since this wasn't the case, I wasn't opening up to anyone other than Aaron. I did have to admit, I was drawn to her a little. She seemed so...happy on the outside. But that panic attack that I knew all too well definitely wasn't the picture of happiness. She had slightly bright red hair, with freckles on her cheeks. Her big hazel eyes looked like they held huge secrets and fears that only she would ever know. Her eyes were what had drawn me in the most. I wanted to figure those secrets out, know what those fears were. Call me crazy, but we all get a little nosy into other's personal lives now and then, don't we? It's not like I would ever see her again after this night. She was Phil Keys' daughter for crying out loud. Bailey was probably touring the world with him, seeing new places, and new things.

They probably lived a filthy rich life with their perfect happy family. At least she wasn't missing her father. She had the perfect family, I didn't. What in the world could she possibly be sad about? "Thanks again, boys! Have a great rest of the night!" my mother yelled into the microphone. They held their beers in the air for a cheers and I faked a smile again at all the men. I couldn't wait to get the hell out of here and forget about this damn night. I was trying to get rid of the emotionally draining sadness always looming in my mind. Who knows what this stupid night could bring back now. There were pictures arranged all over on tables, my Dad's face practically plastered everywhere the firemen could manage to put them. It's like he was just reminding me more and more that he's only a mere picture anymore.

He wasn't coming back. I followed my Mom off stage, grabbing my jacket off the hook on the brick wall of the theatre. Throwing the leathered piece on, I grabbed the keys before my Mom could and she looked up at me curiously. "What are you doing?" she asked, her eyes studying me. "Going for a drive," I stated, playing with the collar of my jacket. "I thought we were leaving as a family..." she said, going to grab the keys from my hand. They jingled a little; making a noise as I quickly pulled them back from her grasp. "Evan Tyler, you give me the keys this instant," she forced, making a move for the keys.

I moved them away from her reach again, sighing. "Mom, I'm not a child anymore. I just need to go for a drive for a few minutes. Clear my head..." I mumbled the last part, looking away from her. I hated talking about emotional bullshit with my Mom; she never said the right things. "How are your brother and I supposed to get home, then?" she inquired, crossing her arms across her chest, giving me the pinching look she always did when I was a kid. "I'll be back in like twenty minutes. Isn't Phil supposed to do an encore anyway?" I asked, referring to the cheers of an encore from the audience of firemen behind us. "He is. But I wanted to get home early. It's way past your brother's bedtime." "Mom, he's ten already. Plus, it's a Friday night. Can't you cut him and me a break for once," I sighed, running my hands through my hair in frustration. She sighed, mimicking my actions and uncrossed her arms, losing the pinched look on her face.

"I suppose I could stay for another half hour or so. Have you've been drinking, Evan?" she asked, the firm tone returning in the question. I froze. How the hell did she know? "Only like one beer, Mom. I'm fine, I swear." I raised my fingers in a Scout's honor position. "Be careful, sweetie. I'm trusting you here. Be back in twenty minutes," she said, holding my gaze. "Yes, mother," I sighed. Even though I was almost twenty one in a month, she still treated me like I was Gregory's age. She kissed my forehead and made her way back to the side-stage as Phil wondered back on with his acoustic guitar in hand. I took a last glance at Bailey, wondering what she was thinking again. I shook my head, and walked towards the nearest exit. Why do I need to be wondering about a girl I barely know?

I dented Mom's car last night. Granted, it was while I was in the middle of having a panic attack from all of the thinking. I had accidentally left my cell phone near my mother's purse and couldn't call Aaron, so I just had to let the freak out happen. I tried pulling over to the side of the road, but some guy came out of nowhere without warning and next thing I knew his front bumper skimmed against my back. Her tail light is kind of cracked and the side of the bumper is a little pushed in, but it's not like anyone had gotten hurt. We had exchanged insurance information and were on our merry way.

I even tried explaining to my Mom about the panic I was in, and she said she felt for me and understood but that I needed to pay for what I had done. She chose the worst thing she could possibly imagine for a twenty year old man like me. She couldn't take away my television privileges or ground me for a month because she knew that would be too much for someone who was of legal age. She made me go to the firehouse with her. Of all the things, she knew this would hurt me the most. She said it wasn't just the denting of her brand new car, but the fact that she had trusted that I only had one beer, when I really had like three. So it was because of the dent in her car and the lies I told her two nights ago that I'm now standing in front of the entrance to the Ladder 24 firehouse. I could practically feel my heart squeezing at the sight, my stomach tied in knots.

I clenched my fists, bracing for another panic. I hated my mother so much right now, and I've never felt this way towards her before. "I hate you so much right now," I mumbled, mimicking my thoughts. She was beside me, holding little Greg's hand. Greg was the complete opposite of me. He was dressed to impress with shades of red and yellow on just like the guys, and had spiked his hair to match my own natural tone. He was smiling big, his eyes wide with excitement. He was used to this, considering they made this a monthly visit. I, on the other hand, was nowhere near excited. "You'll be fine," she sighed, clearly fed up with my behavior at this rate. She smiled down at little Greg and led him away by the hand through the entrance. I swallowed loudly and stuffed my hands in my pockets. I slowly followed behind them, and braced myself for an emotional wreck. It smelled of men's cologne and car wash soap.

Some of the firemen were busy cleaning the big red truck in front of them, whistling to some music coming through a tiny radio off to the side. Others were upstairs, napping, playing card games with their fellow employees, anxiously waiting for a call to help. Little Greg went up to the firemen playing cards and high-fived them all. They had huge smiles plastered on their faces, considering no one could be near my little brother and not smile. They handed him a set of cards and let him join in.

My mother, who dressed nicely for the monthly occasion in a purple and white summer dress with her hair down, walked over to some of Dad's old friends and smiled widely. They greeted her with open arms and began an instant conversation. I was sitting in the middle of the place, taking everything in with open eyes and ears. My mind had fell back to the day my Dad had bought home a similar looking vehicle and what he had told me when he handed it to me. "Whenever you look at that, just know that I'm safe and I'm just protecting all of the people, okay?" I sighed, closing my eyes, taking in the past tense movie playing in my head, remembering his voice to this day, after almost eleven years of him being gone.

"Evan!" my Mom called to me from her stance with the group of guys. I looked over at her and she gestured for me to come over. I sighed heavily, pulling at the ends of my hair as I weaved my hand through it. I walked over to her and stood uncomfortably. "We're really glad to see you, man," one of Dad's old friends said. He was slightly middle-aged, with his dark hair graying. He was muscular and had a firm grip to my hand as he shook it. The rest of them of them nodded or chorused in agreement. "I haven't seen you since you were almost like nine years old!" another man said to me. I smiled at them tightly, nodding my head.

"Sorry it took so long," I said, keeping the conversation short. "You should make this an every month thing, like your mother and brother do," the dark hair man said. I couldn't remember what his name was at all. "You guys know, once a family, always a family, no matter the circumstances." I nodded my head, holding his gaze on me. His words were heartfelt and sincere, but I couldn't be all emotional in that moment. I needed to stay strong for my brother who was only ten feet away from me. "Thanks man, I know," I said. Our heart to heart was interrupted by an immediate chorus of, "Phil!" throughout the station. I turned my head to where everyone was staring and saw Phil Keys in the flesh, sauntering into the station.

He was wearing a light blue button up with light washed jeans, tucked into cowboy boots. He wore a huge smile on his face as he said hello to all the guys coming over to greet him. My gaze fell upon the red hair girl walking behind him though, my breath slightly caught in my throat. She was smiling small, greeting all of the guys who said hello to her after hugging her Dad. She was wearing dark washed skinny jeans, tucked into little boots, with a baby pink off the shoulder shirt on. I watched as she shifted her hair behind her ear, keeping her gaze on the floor, looking almost as uncomfortable as I was.

"Phil Keys is always down here," one of the guys in our group laughed. "Really?" my mother asked, sounding so curious. "Yeah, his father was the old chief and he used to be here all the time as a kid. I just barely met him myself the other night at the show. He's real friendly, that guy." "I left my phone in the car, Mom. I'll be right back," I exclaimed, squeezing her on the shoulder before I made a trek towards the door. I walked past Bailey and outside, leaning against the wall. I breathed a sigh of relief as I ran my hands through my hair, happy to be away from all of the people inside. I looked up at the clouds, taking everything in. I was at my Dad's second home, with all of his friends bombarding me with grief for not being there since he died. How can they blame me? This place just screamed Dad for God's sakes.

I heard the sound of the glass door closing and looked over my shoulder. "Sorry," she mumbled. She made a quick glance towards the door and went to walk back inside. "Why do we keep meeting up like this?" I laughed slightly, looking over at her. She smiled a little at my laughter and turned back around to lean against the wall with me. She stayed a few ways away, knowing we weren't quite friends. "I hate when everyone bombards me with questions all the time. Especially about my sister," she rambled, looking past me as she spoke. "Ah, so you do have a sister, then?" I asked, raising an eyebrow. Her cheeks turned that shade of baby pink again, matching her shirt. She glanced down at the ground before I could read how she felt.

A few moments of silence fell through the air as she stared at the ground and I looked up at the sky. I still wondered what she was all about, and why she couldn't even speak to me about her sister. "Why don't you like to talk about your-" I went to ask, but she cut me off. "So why are we meeting like this again?" she looked up at me with those big hazel eyes again, studying me. "I hate getting questions from them too," I said, staring back at her. "Why'd you come then?" she asked.

Her one thumb was looped through the belt loop of her jeans as she leaned against the brick siding of the station. I could sense the small bit of country girl in her from that action. "Why'd you come?" I inquired back, looking over at her. She looked up at me and smiled gently. "I asked you first." "My Mom dragged me here," I huffed, running a hand through my hair. I still needed to pay her back for the car. Even though I felt like this was enough pay back as it was.

"Same with my Dad," she sighed. She went to move a piece of hair behind her ear again and her tattoo that I had noticed two nights ago came back into view. "You still never told me what that tattoo meant..." I said, gauging her reaction.

She froze slightly, just like she had that night. I could practically see the emotional wall going back up, ending our light conversation. "I don't have to tell you what it means at all," she said roughly, giving me a glare before throwing her hair behind her shoulder as she turned away from me and walked towards the door. I watched as she walked through the door and let it slam shut behind her, leaving me at the wall by myself again.

What the hell was that all about? If you didn't want others asking you about your tattoo, then don't get it plastered boldly onto your wrist where everyone can view it. Others will obviously ask you about it if it comes up in conversation. I ask a question and I'm suddenly the bad guy. Maybe it's best that I don't get to know this girl then.

Chapter 7

Maybe I was being rude. I didn't care in that moment. I didn't owe Evan any source of explanation because I barely knew the guy. I barely let my old friends in, let alone some boy. This was what I did best. I pushed others away, not showing how much someone meant to me, because I was too scared of getting hurt again. I probably shouldn't have gotten the tattoo plastered onto a spot on my body where others would obviously see and be utterly curious about.

But it was my physical way of showing how much Lanie meant to me. The sisterly bond we shared before she died is something her and I will ever understand. Or I guess in her case...understood. I shook my head lightly at myself, trying to shake the slight guilt I felt for being so rude to Evan. It's not like he deserved to be talked to like that. I could have stayed and tried to drive the conversation in a separate direction, but I knew how he would react. He would try to pry more into my personal life than he knew better of.

Everyone always did that, which was why I became so good at pushing the ones I loved out of my life. My parents sure taught me well. "Bailey, you ready to get out of here?" my father smiled down at me, while standing around in a circle with some of Grandpa's old friends. I nodded my head lightly, not giving too much eye contact.

I just needed to get the hell out of here and get back into my bed. Lanie's bed. My Dad looped his keys around his fingers a couple of times, shaking hands and hugging some of his old buddies and we headed to the car.

"God, I sure do love that place," he drawled, turning up the radio to his favorite rock station. It signaled that he definitely didn't want to continue a conversation with me. I was just the only person he could give his opinions to, since Lanie wasn't around any longer and my mother was off doing legal business as usual.

I rested my head against the window and watched as the trees and yellow street lines flourished through my eyesight. I couldn't wait to be away from this city, start fresh, and not have to see Lanie's favorite places or things everywhere I looked. I especially couldn't wait to be away from my parents. I know they damn well couldn't wait to get away from me.

As I lay in bed that night, I replayed the two conversations Evan and I have had in the past week or so. For some reason I couldn't shake the familiarity I felt around him. I felt as though someone might finally be able to stand sitting in a conversation with me without disliking me for once. I felt the small amount of guilt creep up in my stomach again and it almost made me feel sick. Maybe I was too much of a pushover, or maybe I was too nice. But, I felt like I sort of owed Evan an apology of some sort. I was never that mean to a person, especially someone who didn't deserve it. "Lane," I whispered, looking up at her old ceiling. It had yellow stars painted on in the center with a midnight blue and black mixture of colors surrounding it.

My Dad had painted them on for Lanie when she was about six, because she loved lying down and looking up at the stars outside.

She believed there was a whole world ahead of her, no matter how old she got. She knew she could explore the world and do anything she wanted. And whenever she felt the slightest bit down, which clearly wasn't often, she would look up and know that she was one in a massive expanse of people and that she wasn't alone. The colors didn't make me feel that way tonight. They just made me feel more alone. I sighed, staring up at the ceiling. "I miss you so much. But, you already know that because I tell you this like every single night," I said, smiling slightly. I pushed a piece of reddish hair away from my face and continued.

"You saw how big of a bitch I was to that guy? God, he didn't deserve that. I mean, he was only curious. About you, basically. But, who wasn't ever curious about you? Especially when it came to guys. Maybe I was scared, I don't know. Maybe I was scared that he could see through me somehow. I don't want to let anyone else in Lane. I let you in, and look what happened. You were my best friend. You were the basic definition of a best friend," I laughed a little.

"Can't you make everything better, up there?" I sighed. "I need some happiness Lane. I'm so sick and tired of being sad all of the time. I'm not blaming you at all; I just...can't seem to function without you here anymore. It's been two years, and you'd think I'd moved on already. I haven't moved on Lanie. You were the better half of me. No one likes me here. I made friends because of you. How am I supposed to function now?" I shook my head, noticing a small drop of water cascade onto the pillow underneath my head. I always cried when I tried talking to her. My brain still didn't want to believe that she was gone. She literally was my better half. How do you move on from someone who you relied on for everything?

How do you confide in someone other than your best friend, your sister? "Come back Lanie."

I breathed, letting the tears fall freely as I felt my heart squeeze with utter sadness. I couldn't do this without her. I couldn't do it.

"Bailey!" I heard my mother call my name later on, waking me up from the depressive slumber. My eyes were swollen shut, and I knew my cheeks were still red. I had just fallen asleep for about thirty minutes or so, and she was waking me up already. I sighed heavily and pulled a pair of polka-dotted pajama shorts on. "Bailey Renee!" she practically spat as loudly as she could. It was almost midnight, it was not necessary to scream like that at this late hour. "I'm coming!" I shouted. I purposefully let my steps become slower as I made my way through the large house, down the stairs. My feet meshed with the white plush carpet beneath my feet as I skidded through the living room and to the kitchen where I heard my mother call my name for what felt like the tenth time. I pushed open the massive swinging wooden door and was met with blank expressions from both my mother and father as they were sat at the dining table. My Dad had his hands crossed in front of him, looking over to my mother to begin speaking.

What the hell was going on? "Sit, Bailey," my Mom urged, throwing an arm in the direction of the chair across from her. I eyed her weirdly and slowly sat down, facing them both with an anxious, but worried expression on my face. "What did I do?" I asked nervously. As I awaited their response, my leg bounced anxiously beneath the table. "Your father and I are worried about you," she said, slowly and carefully, gauging my reaction. I'm telling you, if it was physically possible for my eyeballs to popping out of my sockets right now like in cartoons, they would be.

"You've got to be fucking kidding me," I said quickly, without bothering to refrain to PG language. "Language," my mother snapped. "We're worried because you've been cooped up in her room since God only knows when, and have yet to go see your friends or see a building other than our home." What friends, I thought. I eyed her carefully, trying to figure out where the hell all of this was coming from.

"We've gotten you a job," she continued, looking over at my father for reinforcement. He only nodded along to what she said, looking over at me. He never read any emotion of the sort since the day Lanie died, and he still hadn't right now. "What?" I exclaimed. "We're tired of seeing you cooped in that dreaded room of hers and want you to see the light of day once in a while," she continued. I laughed a little in front of her, my shoulders actually shaking. I did this for two reasons. One, she couldn't even say Lanie's name since the day she passed away and it was like she was forbidden to even be spoken of in this house. My second reason was because she actually pretended to care about my well being. This was all definitely new to me.

"We've gotten you a job at the theatre that your father played at for the benefit," she continued, talking over my silent laughing. I loved how she carried on a discussion with me using "We" over and over, when my Dad hadn't said a word since I walked down here. "Are you on drugs?" I stated, blankly. She gasped loudly and scolded me for my attitude. I didn't care at that point. How dare they pretend like they cared about my well being and what I was doing all day? She was too busy carrying on her new law firm and my Dad was practically never home. Since when did what I was doing mean anything to them? "No, how dare you guys. No one gave a flying fuck what I was doing since the day that Lanie died." Mom's eyes bulged at the mention of Lanie's name. My Dad still looked blankly on in the midst of the conversation.

"Yeah that's right, I said her name. Lanie!" I shouted. "Lanie, Lanie, Lanie! I'm so sick of pretending like her name is forbidden in this house. She existed mother, and I know that you know that. She was your favorite daughter. You spent every waking hour obsessing over her. Stop pretending like you hadn't. She died! That doesn't mean that we don't continue to talk about her anymore!" I had my hands flying all over the place and I was suddenly pacing the kitchen back and forth.

"Now Bailey," my Dad started. I cut him off immediately. "Oh, the silent man speaks!" I yelled, throwing my hands in the air. He went to speak again, and I put a hand up to stop him. "No! I have yet to finish Dad! Another thing, how dare you both suddenly pick an interest in my life and set me up with a job without even asking what I wanted to do. You don't get to push into my life all of the sudden without even giving the slightest hint of worrying about it before! You guys don't care about me. All you cared about was her!" I pointed up at the sky, referring to my long lost older sister, my chest heaving from the exertion of yelling and the emotions all tumbling out at once. "We-" my mother began, but I conveniently cut her off again with the raise of a hand.

"Be quiet, mother. Stop saying we when Dad hasn't said a single fucking word since I walked into this kitchen. You're both the worst parents I could possibly imagine having. If Lanie was clearly the favorite, why did you both bother creating me? When I know I'm such a burden to take care of!" I couldn't take it all anymore so I stomped off, out of the kitchen, letting the door swing roughly back and forth behind me. I heaved in heavy breaths as I made my way back upstairs and into the bedroom that I knew so well. I fell back onto the bed, trying to compose myself. I felt like a small amount of weight was lifted off of my shoulders, but I knew for a fact that my words hadn't affected my parents at all.

But then I heard a knock at the door. Maybe I did have an affect on them? I wasn't risking having to look my mother in the eye again so I called out to the door from my bed. "Yes?" "You're Mom sent me up here," my Dad called through the door. He sounded sullen and I was suddenly very curious as to what his face portrayed at that moment. I wondered if my words had gotten to him. I wondered if he actually showed emotion for once in his life on that scruffy, graying face. "And?" I prodded, sitting up slightly in the bed.

"She said your new job starts tomorrow and to be in by ten in the morning. If you don't show up..." he took in a breath for a second. "We'll find out and you'll be grounded." I stared wide-eyed at the door and listened as his massive foot steps turned away from my bedroom door and down the stairs to that dreaded woman in the kitchen. And to think, I actually thought my words had finally gotten to them. Maybe I actually got through their heads how lost I felt, how unwanted I felt in this home. I thought that at the most, one of them would understand how much I wanted to feel like their daughter again. I was so, so wrong.

Chapter 8

" Evan! Sweetie, have you seen my cell phone?" my Mom called upstairs to me. I was on my laptop, perched at the head of my bed, looking for online classes I could take. Or maybe an actual college would cut it too.

I had started college at eighteen like any usual kid my age would have done if they wanted to become something in their future. The thing was though, three months into it and I was writhing in pain from the anxiety I was experiencing with work loads, worrying about my Mom and little brother, and having college debt pile up in six digit figures. I'd so badly wanted to become a psychologist type person for kids who suffered from deaths in their family.

It was my dream to help kids who were like me at the mere age of ten who lost a parent, or even someone they loved. I wanted to be what I didn't have at that age. At the time, Mom was too self-involved with her own grief, and with little Greg on the way, therapists just weren't in the cards for me. The budget wasn't cut for therapist bills, because baby Greg still needed to be taken care of. So, as I grew up, I used my own self therapeutic ways to get me by. I would shoot things with bb guns in the woods with Aaron.

At thirteen I developed an interest in heavy breakdowns and hardcore screaming music that I would blast all throughout the day. But, as I got older, I toned down the punk look and put down the mini guns and just started staring up at the stars in the field behind my house. That would probably sound incredibly pansy like to any guy that you told, which is part of the reason why I didn't tell any of my friends aside from Aaron, but I did it to clear my head.

I thought maybe, in some way, my Dad was up there, watching over what I was doing. Maybe he was leading in me in the right path or something. Now, though, I'm trying to get back into school so I can make something of myself. I'm going to be twenty-one soon, a legal adult, and I have nothing to show for it but a piece of paper that says I completed high school. Who the hell would want to hire me with just that? I didn't even know what I wanted to do at this point.

As much as I wanted to be a child psychologist, I knew that I just didn't have the money for it right now, and seven or eight years of schooling would be a whole hell of a lot. Plus, that would mean that I couldn't actually begin my career until well into my twenty-eighth birthday, which was a little too late in life for me. I wanted to start something early, that I could see myself doing when I was at a really old age. I wanted to become something my Dad would be proud, something I would be proud of. I wanted to earn my own living and have something to show for it. I just wish I could figure out what it was.

All I knew was that I needed to give my Mom back something. She's done enough for me as it is, and it's time I give back. "No?" I shouted down to her. "I thought you've had it?" "I haven't seen it since…oh no, I think I left it at the theatre," she said, sounding sullen. Someone definitely had to have picked it up by now. There had to been at the least ten shows since the Phil show, so someone could have taken it as their own by this point. "Crap," I said, getting up and setting my laptop on the sheets. I opened my door and walked to the top of the stairs. I looked down at my Mom who was contemplating on what to do.

"I need that phone for my work contacts. I can't maintain all of the paper work without that phone," she mumbled, mostly to herself. My mother worked as a social worker from home, and kept most of her contacts in this special filing app that she had on her new phone. She said it helped her when she could just speak into the phone and tell them the name, so it would pop up and call it for her. She said it was a time saver or something, and it was better than a huge contact book in paper. "Well do you want me to go look for you?" I asked, feeling like I needed to help her in some way. She's always so flustered now. Her eyes lit up as she looked up at me. "Oh, would you Evan? That would help me out a lot." "Sure thing. Just leave me the keys and I'll go throw on some shoes."

Twenty agonizing traffic filled minutes later, and I was at the theatre. I parked Mom's car over in the abandoned parking area and clicked the switch to lock it up. There were no cars around, considering it was mid-morning and shows were usually happening at night. I walked through the familiar glass doors and looked over to see a girl with blonde, bouncy curls was wiping off a beer glass at the bar. "Can I help you?" she called to me, looking up at the chime from the door I'd just walked through. "Yeah, uh have you guys seen a random phone lying around here? It's that new Nokia phone, all square and stuff with a pink case," I said, making my way over to the bar. I remembered this girl.

She'd served me the couple bottles of beer, while I flirted with her for a few minutes. The only reason I did was to get the beers, not get anything from her. But she was hot and around my age so I figured I could work to get what I wanted. "Oh, I remember you," she murmured, looking up at me, batting her heavily coated eyelashes. She had on a white button-up and black pants, but the buttons were a little too undone at the top, exposing a decent amount of her chest. She leaned over the bar, trying to gauge my attention in the best way she could think of. I looked down at her chest for a brief moment, a little distracted, and cleared my throat. I needed to remember why I was here. "And I remember you," I countered. "But, have you seen the phone?" I leaned my arms on the bar, coming face to face with her.

She blushed a little, not used to the close contact. I grinned devilishly, liking that I could make her blush. "Someone must have found the phone you're looking for. Is it your girlfriend's?" she prodded, clearly asking for her own benefit. "Nope," I said, popping the 'p'. "It's my mother's." "Oh, I see. So no girlfriend, then?" she asked, leaning closer, exposing more of her chest. "Leslie have you seen the…" I heard an all too familiar voice coming from the door behind the blonde. I took my eyes away from the gorgeous girl in front of me to see who it was. My eyes widened a little, matching hers. "Bailey?" She looked like a deer caught in the headlights, and she blushed at my voice. "Sorry. I didn't mean to interrupt. Leslie, I just need…" she looked over at Leslie, trying not to make eye contact with me again.

"How do you guys know each other?" Leslie prodded more. She looked between me and Bailey and raised a thin, blonde eyebrow. "We met here the night of the Phil concert," I exclaimed, never taking my eyes off of the red head in front of me. She was looking everywhere but at me, and keeping her fingers busy with rearranging beer bottles. "Oh! That's...cool, I guess," Leslie's voice faded, like she had been a little intimidated. She must have thought something was going on with Bailey. "What did you need, Bailey?" she asked. Bailey raised her eyes to meet Leslie's and she seemed at a lose for words. "Um...the uh, extension cord," she chirped, playing with the hem of her white button-up, similar to Leslie's. "Dan said he needs it for some amp work or something?" "Right here!" she exclaimed, searching under the bar for a couple of seconds to lift up the orange piece of wiring. "Here you go," she said, handing it to Bailey. She still hadn't looked me in the eye since she realized who I was. "Thanks," she mumbled. "I'll leave you guys be, then," she continued, turning towards the door and letting it swing shut behind her. "So, I was thinking..." Leslie said, looking up at me with those flirtatious eyes again. "Uh, I'll be right back," I told her, going around the bar, and following wherever Bailey had gone.

I heard Leslie yell something like, "Hey, you can't go through there," but I ignored her and kept on walking. I made my way through a hallway, with a door that was opened, exposing a massive amount of sunlight. I figured she had walked through there, so I made my way outside, and noticed a small stage set up. A large man, who looked middle-aged, was knelt in front of an amp, with his back to me. I didn't pay too much attention to him though, because I noticed the red haired girl I'd been looking for and I walked over to touch her arm. She jumped at the sudden contact and turned around, wide-eyed. "Can we talk?" I whispered, not wanting to get the old man's attention. She merely nodded and told the guy she was going on break for a few minutes.

"Just a few minutes, Bail. I need you to help set the rest of this stage up before tonight," he told her in a gruff voice, not looking up from his place on the floor. "Okay," she called to him, as she guided me around the outside of the building, to a clear opening, with a field behind it. The grass seemed to go on forever, and there was a patio with a table and chair set propped on the cement. "Damn, I didn't even know this was back here," I breathed, looking all the way down to where the grass expansion stopped at a river, with trees lining the sides of it. "Yeah, it's the 'break room,'" she said, using air quotes.

"It's pretty nice back here." "It is," I mimicked. I turned around to look at her eyes and she seemed like she couldn't look at me. "Okay, I'm sorry for being such a nosy asshole to you the day at the station. I'm not usually like that," I rambled. I'd felt like shit since the day that I prodded into her personal life, even though I knew it wasn't entirely my fault. I felt like she wouldn't have run off so fast if I hadn't been pushy.

"It's fine," she sighed. "I was the one being an ass," she commented, finally looking up at me with those big, hazel eyes. Her freckles were more noticeable as the sun shone from behind me, onto her cheeks. Her light red hair was curled into waves around her face, and pushed to one side of her head. I hated her uniform though, because it was so generic and made her look a little bigger than I remembered her being.

"You weren't. I mean, I shouldn't have prodded into your life like that. We barely know each other. It's none of my business," I rambled on more. I just wanted this girl to talk to me. I'd never had trouble talking to girls before now, and she was making me want to speak to her more and more as the days went on. "It's okay," she said, touching my arm. I felt a slight warm feeling creep up at the spot and wondered what the hell was going on with me. "Seriously. It's over with." "Good," I smiled down at her, noticing she was actually looking up at me for once with a grin playing at her lips. "Now why are you here?" she asked, crossing her arms.

"I feel like this is a repeat from a few days ago," I laughed. She smiled at me, but waited for my response. "I'm here to find my Mom's phone. It's a Nokia with a little-" She cut me off. "A little pink case around it?" she finished for me. I widened my eyes. "You have it?" I asked, releasing a breath, knowing I wouldn't have to go home empty handed, with a brooding, freaked out mother on my hands.

"Mhm," she stated. "It's in the owner's office though. I can tell you where it is," she went off, giving me directions on rights and lefts, with which door to look out for. "Thanks," I stated, grinning. I went to walk around her, silently hating myself for not wanting to leave just yet. "Hey, Bailey?" I asked, turning back around to her again. "Yeah?" she asked, looking up at me with those big eyes again.

"Would you want to maybe...hang out sometime?" I asked, warily. I was anxiously awaiting her answer as her eyes bulged. Crap, she probably thought I was completely ridiculous. We barely even knew each other, why would she want to hang out with someone like me? "Uh, sure," she said, nervously. She bit down on her lip and I refrained myself from looking down at it. What the hell was going on with me? "Meet me at this spot tomorrow night at around 9?" she finished.

"Sounds good to me," I grinned at her, liking the blush I put onto her face. "See you then." "Yeah, see you then," she smiled, waving at me before I walked back around the building, and back inside. Things might turn out alright after all.

Chapter 9

I hadn't faltered the smile on my face all day long. It was amazing how one person could completely turn your day around with a few simple words or a simple question. Maybe Lanie had finally listened to me after all, and things might actually begin to fall back together. I twirled around in my room, listening to some new rock band on the radio, and flipped through the many outfits squished together in my closet, trying to find something not too subtle, but not too slutty either. I didn't know the type of girls Evan liked, and I didn't want to turn his thoughts in the opposite direction.

"Thanks for this, Lane," I whispered, looking up at the ceiling, trying to talk to her again. "I knew you would help me out somehow," I smiled. I finally settled on a white, above the knee, stitched dress, with a bow to tie the middle. I sat in front of my mirror, applying a layer of mascara, and light shade of foundation, perfecting my skin. I was laying low on the makeup, as I curled my light red hair in loose ringlets to frame my face. I've never had an actual date like this before. Sure, there were boys that I had hooked up with at parties when Lanie was around. But, ever since she died, I hadn't gotten out much, aside from my job at the theatre, and Dad's concert. This left little room for boys and dates.

I didn't want to say that I was anti-social in anyway, I just wasn't up for making new friends at this point. I was going away to university soon, and I didn't want attachments to keep me behind. But, the part I knew was creeping up was telling me that the only reason why I really wasn't out much anymore was because I did it to myself. I pushed all of my friends away after Lanie passed, because I couldn't handle all of the pitying looks anymore. Who wants to be stared at like some worthless sad puppy all the time? I sure didn't. It also was based around the fact that Lanie made most of my friends for me. Everyone I knew, she introduced me to.

She was always popular in school, and knew every person in every grade. The boys drooled over her and the girls wanted to be her. She wasn't one to have a new boyfriend every week, more like every year. But as soon as she broke up with the old guy, a new one would swoop in and fall to her feet. It was like she had this power over the people around her and that no one could understand. If she smiled, giggled, or even flipped her over her shoulder, she had grabbed someone's attention and kept them at her reach for as long as she needed to. I, on the other hand, was too shy to start up a conversation on my own, and boys would barely even look in my direction when I walked down the hallways at school. In the beginning years of high school, I wore glasses and had frizzy hair, with unattractive freckles lining my cheeks.

All of this was before I discovered hair products and makeup, but that still didn't seem like enough to impress everyone like Lanie did. I was the complete opposite of my sister. And I was always left feeling like I could never measure up to her. My best friends were even friends with her before they were with me. They weren't close like we were, but she practically knew everyone so it was a given. When she went away to college, she left them behind because they were in my grade and I was left with three new best friends, Annabelle, Maisey and Lily. We'd go to parties together, shop together, and have movie nights and long heart to hearts at sleepovers. We were inseparable.

But, when she died, I didn't know how to cope. So I stopped answering messages, phone calls, and knocks at the door, just to make it all go away. They didn't take my ignoring them too well and I was often called a self-centered bitch by them, or so I was told by the numerous whispers around me at school. I wasn't trying to hurt anyone's feelings. I was trying to protect my own well being. That may have been selfish, but I was putting my own feelings aside for years, and it was time for me to step up to the plate now that Lanie was gone. I couldn't stand to be around people anymore.

What was the point in being close to someone when they would be taken away from you sooner or later? I didn't want attachments before going away, but somehow Evan made me think differently. I didn't know how this was going to go. We could end up as friends for all I knew. I just knew that I was finally comfortable around someone other than Lanie in silence, and this was all new to me. I didn't know what it was about Evan, but I felt drawn to him in the weirdest, most oddly comforting way a person could be. Even though we were almost strangers, it was like a certain pull had made me want to know him more. The only thing I was unsure about was letting him in on my own life. I wasn't too keen on letting someone else in, especially when it came to Lanie.

I never did, and still don't like crying or letting my emotions out to other people. It felt like I was losing my wall that I had taken so long to build up when it came to confronting others. I didn't like drama, or hysterics, and if I really needed to unload, Lanie was always there, with open ears, ready to let me have it. Now, with Lanie gone, I didn't feel comfortable letting anyone else in. What if something happened to them? What if they didn't like the real me, and decided to just up and leave me when I needed them the most? I couldn't handle anymore goodbyes. I hadn't told my parents where I was going, because we hadn't spoken to each other ever since the fight in the kitchen.

My Dad was whipped to the biggest degree, and my mother was the pure definition of a bitch. She was up in her bed, reading some type of book on law and regulations, and Dad was in his study, strumming away on his guitar. They wouldn't even notice if I was gone for two days, let alone a few hours. At this point, I couldn't wait to be away at university, living my own life, without feeling like I was a big burden on everyone in this house. So, I quietly picked up my heels and tip-toed down the plush stairs, and lightly shut the door behind me. I slipped on my black heels and got to my car, pulling out of the driveway as quietly as possible. I couldn't fight the smile on my face as I made my way down the street, towards the backyard of the theatre where I was supposed to meet rooftop boy.

I don't know what it was, but I was finally feeling wanted in a way. Someone actually wanted to spend time with me, listen to what I had to say. I didn't feel like I was burdening him, because I hadn't asked for the date, he had. After I reached the parking lot, I made sure to lock my car door, walking through the dark night towards the beautiful backyard of the theatre, taking a seat in the white, plastic porch chair, and looked up at the stars. I didn't want to lie down in the grass in a white dress, but I did the second best thing that brought me close to Lanie. I was relaxed, up until the point where I checked my phone and it said that it was quarter after ten, and I had been sitting here for over an hour.

I tried to push down the hurt that I knew was bubbling in my stomach, knowing I'd been stood up. Maybe, I wasn't as wanted as I thought. I didn't let myself over think the matter, and I just kept my eyes fixated on the stars above me. I was silently crossing my fingers that this wouldn't be a bust, and everything was going to turn out okay for once. I could give it a little time, I could wait it out. Everything was going to be okay. I gave it another twenty minutes, and when I hadn't even heard the slightest noise of a car pulling up out front, I picked up my bag and searched for my keys. I rapidly wiped under my eyes, trying not to smudge the makeup I had on. It wasn't like it mattered at this point anyway; no one was here to see it. Then I heard a gruff boy's voice and stopped dead in the midst of my hands in my bag.

"Bailey!" I heard him yell. "Oh, Bailey!" he wailed. No he wasn't... "Evan?" I asked, getting up from my seat. I watched the corner of the building, waiting for him to turn around the way. My eyes widened as I took him in. He was walking sloppily around the corner, with his leather jacket slightly hanging off of one shoulder. He had on a light blue t-shirt with noticeable wet stains printed on the front, and jeans without a belt, making his pants sag a little. His usually nicely styled black hair was in a messy heap on top of his head, some of it getting in his eyes.

"Heyyyy," he slurred, blowing up at the little piece of hair in his eye. He giggled slightly as the hair blew up, but unsuccessfully fell back into his eyes. "I'm here!" he bellowed, throwing his hands unsteadily up in the air. I couldn't walk any closer and stood in the same spot I began with, in front of the chair and table, waiting for him to come closer. He couldn't be drunk. This just didn't need to happen right now. He wobbled over to me, almost tripping over his own footing. He giggled a little at himself again, before catching on and pulling himself back up. "So what's up?" he said, swaying a little. Before he fell to his side again, I pulled him up and steadied him by his arms.

"Are you drunk?" I asked, already knowing my answer. He reeked of alcohol, and I had to turn my head away slightly when he opened his mouth to answer me. "Mm, nope!" he laughed. "Don't think so," he pondered for a moment, putting a finger to his chin sloppily. "I think you are," I sighed. He almost fell again and I walked him over to the grass expansion, before he smacked his head on the concrete below us. I let him go and he slammed his butt on the grass and lied back. I stood over him, watching him as he blinked slowly, staring up at the stars. I was filled with so many different emotions in that moment, that I didn't know how to handle myself, or even Evan for that matter.

I was hurt, angry, confused, and scared as to how he even ended up here being the drunken mess that he was. "Sit," he exclaimed, patting the area of grass next to him. I shook my head at him, at a loss for words. He pouted, his plump lower lip protruding more. "I can't believe this," I sighed to myself, looking up at the sky. "I suck, don't I?" he laughed at himself, throwing a muscled arm over his eyes. "You do," I agreed. I crossed my arms over my chest, not really bothered by the light breeze forming around us. It calmed me down, but only a little. I silently prayed that those pesky tears wouldn't betray me and show how hurt I was. He actually needed to be drunk to go on a date with me.

That must make a person feel so special. "Are you crying?" he asked, his voice light. I sighed again, hating that I let a few reach my lids. I wiped quickly at them, and shook my head. I didn't dare meet his glazed over eyes, and kept fixed up at the stars above us. "I'm sorry," he pouted again. "I fuck up too much," he noted, shaking his head. "It's fine," I breathed, not trusting my voice at a normal level. "I think I'm going to go." I wasn't about to make him my responsibility.

We didn't know each other well, and we didn't even count as friends. At this point, I didn't even want a friendship with this asshole. Who asks a girl on a date, only to show up drunk and partially incoherent? Was there a point to that? "No," he whimpered. Without getting up, he reached his hand up in a 'come back' motion. I looked down at him, shaking my head. "How did you even get here?" I asked, crossing my arms again. "Drove," he stated simply, like it wasn't a big deal in his condition. "You're kidding me right?!" I shouted at him. He winced, closing his eyes.

"Sh, Bailey. Don't scream," he said, waving his hands. "How the hell did you drive like that?" I asked, my voice not losing its tone. He gave me a drunken smile like he was proud. "I'm an awesome drunk driver." I rolled my eyes, getting too fed up with him at this point. I don't why I felt so drawn to him. Right now, I could care less if I ever saw him again. "I'm leaving, Evan," I stated, shaking my head, throwing my hands down in frustration. "No!" he called to me, but I didn't stop this time. When he watched me retreating further away from him, I heard him yell. "God, I'm such a fuck up! Ever since you died, Dad, I can't do anything right anymore," he growled, throwing his hands over his eyes. I stopped dead in my tracks, turning around slowly. His Dad died? "Why'd you have to go and die on me, huh? You couldn't wait till you were old and shit to leave me? I might have handled it better!" he shouted towards the sky.

He must have thought I left, because he kept yelling up at the sky, like I always did when talking to Lanie. He wasn't talking to me at all. "Leave me with all the responsibilities! Good idea, Dad! You didn't even meet Greg," he cried out, rubbing his fists viciously over his eyes. I watched with wide eyes at the confession spilling from his lips. It all started to add up to me. This was why he froze up when I asked about him being a firefighter's son, why when they talked about him in the speech, he was nowhere to be seen. This was why he had a foundation in his name.

I walked over to him slowly, discarding my heels on the pavement and sinking my feet into the plush grass beneath me. I didn't care about my dress, or how dirty I knew it was going to get if I sat on the grass for too long. I sunk down next to Evan, who was still shouting up at the sky. I noticed how his voice cracked slightly, the more confessions that left his lips.

"Why'd you do that, Dad? Why didn't you stay?" he pleaded, his voice becoming rougher and more cracked as he continued. He rubbed his eyes roughly again, and it looked like he was trying to keep the tears away. He was completely breaking down in front of me, and I didn't know what to do. I just felt my heart breaking into pieces as I watched this perfect looking guy crumble next to me. How long had he been keeping this stuff in? "Evan," I said, tentatively. I put my hand over one of his that was still rubbing at his face. He took it away from his eyes and looked up at me, eyes still glazed over and slightly watery. They were red rimmed and puffy and he looked like he was in so much pain in that moment.

I just intertwined my fingers with his and lied back, staring up at the stars with him. "Why did he have to leave so damn early?" he choked. "Who does that!" "It's out of our hands. It happens to so many other people. They think they should stay, but it's not up to us," I said softly, still holding onto his hand. We didn't look at each other as we spoke, just kept staring up at the dark sky above us. "That's so fucked up," he scoffed, shaking his head back and forth. "Who could take away someone who was so young and had so much life left to live?" "Fate's an asshole," I stated, knowing exactly how he felt. When Lanie died, I always kept questioning why someone could be taking away a person who was so young.

Some people were still so young, or so genuine, or so kind. Why take away the good in this world? What good did that do for the world? Their families needed them. Kids needed their parents. Parents needed their children. Even parents still needed their parents. It was all apart of life, but not a part of life that I liked at all. What was the point of putting someone in your life, only to take them away not too long after? He laughed slightly, still in his drunken state. "No shit," he said. "My little brother needs his Dad," he exclaimed simply. "I'm not good enough to be his Dad, no matter what I do." It was so strange to me how I barely knew this boy and he was baring his soul to me. He knew nothing about me, or I him.

Maybe it was the alcohol making him warm up to me more. Maybe he was too tired to put a wall around anyone anymore. All I knew was that I wasn't going to leave him here like this. He obviously needed someone to let it all out to, even if he did regret it in the morning. "You're really nice, you know that," he screeched, his tone sounding slightly baby-fied. "No one ever really listens to me, 'cept my Mom." "You're...welcome?" I questioned, smiling lightly at him. I was guessing that the heart to heart was over and the silly drunk boy was back beneath the barrier. "And you're really pretty, too," he screeched again, throwing an arm over his eyes. I only smiled in response, looking over at his hiding face.

"Your friend is hot though," he slurred. "The one at the bar..." he mumbled. "Leslie...?" I questioned, feeling my heart skip a beat. "Yeah, that blonde one," he pointed a sloppy finger back towards the building behind us. "You should set me up with her!" he gasped, looking over at me with playful eyes. I felt bad butterflies make their way into my stomach as I replayed what he said in my head. I don't know why it hurt, I didn't know him. I think I was expecting too much from someone who was a stranger. It didn't matter that he found comfort in confiding in me. He probably wasn't going to remember this come morning, and I shouldn't be over-thinking everything all the time.

"Will do," I sighed, letting my fingers slip from his. I stayed there, looking up at the stars, wishing again that Lanie was here. She would tell me to stop over-thinking everything and just be friends with the guy. She would say to stop being such a baby, in a joking way of course, and let things be.

She always seemed to be an expert in fate, except when it came to her life being in the hands of it. It was only a few minutes later that I heard Evan snore lightly, lying on his back still. He was winding down from all the alcohol and I was winding down from the hundreds of emotions playing around in my mind. It wasn't that long later that I felt myself drifting off as well, next to the odd guy next to me, in the grassy expansion behind the theatre. Life works in mysterious ways, I guess.

Chapter 10

When I woke up, I was seeing green. Literally. My face was smothered in this patch of green stuff. I didn't even know what was going on. My head was spinning and I honestly thought I was hallucinating. My eyes were wincing at the light when I turned my head and was met with the brightest fucking sun I've ever seen in my life. My room was never this bright, what the hell was going on? I went to go rub my eyes and noticed that my hand was tightly clutching someone else's. I turned my head slowly and saw the familiar looking red head sleeping soundly next to me, her hand not even leaving mine.

What the fuck happened last night? She was lying on her side, one hand underneath her head, and the other holding onto mine. Her light red hair was falling in her eyes and her makeup look like it had been running. I let go of her hand and sat up on my elbows. I was sitting in a huge field of grass and the sun was bright as hell. I shielded my wincing eyes with an arm and I could practically smell the alcohol on my jacket. Did I spill the whole bottle on myself last night in the process? Shit. Last night.

I was supposed to be hanging out with the sleeping girl next to me last night. As the events of last night rushed back to me, I fell onto my back and closed my eyes. I felt like I needed a drink so

I took a shot of Jack Daniels before I was about to leave. I was dressed and ready to go, but the alcohol seemed to call me back and I kept telling myself, 'one more shot'. I couldn't remember what happened after the third glass, and I didn't think I wanted to at this point. I looked over at Bailey still silently sleeping next to me and I felt like the hugest ass in the world right now. I must have come to see her after handling the bottle on my own. She was expecting the guy she met before, and I definitely wasn't my usual self.

Can't say I didn't warn her though. I did things like this all the time. I was an asshole, and I knew that too well. Sure, I did nice things for my mom, or for little Greg sometimes, but I always managed to fuck something up in the process. To say my chances with Bailey were probably gone was an understatement.

My head was pounding as I massaged my temple. It was way too bright out here for someone with a massive hangover and I wasn't about to sit out here all day long. I needed to get home. I reached into my pocket for my phone, clicking the unlock button, waiting for the time to pop up. It was eight in the morning and I had two missed calls from my mom and a text from little Greg. I smiled as I read it, because he was asking where I was because I was supposed to read him his bedtime story. I winced though, because that little pang of guilt spread up in me, knowing I happened to let my little brother down...again.

I heard Bailey stir beside me and looked over at her. She rubbed her eyes and opened them slowly. Her hazel eyes shown bright as she widened them, taking in the setting around her. "Holy crap," she murmured, finally looking over at me. Her eyes were wide like a kid in shock and I chuckled slightly. "About the same response I had when I woke up," I said, putting my hands underneath my head. "I'm sorry. I didn't want to...uh, leave you alone, in the state that you were in," she said, sitting up on her elbows. She wiped underneath her eyes with a single finger and frowned when she noticed all of the black from the smudges on her face.

"Thanks for that, by the way. I know I must have been an asshole last night," I faded off, closing my eyes from the pain in my head. "It's okay," she whispered, sighing afterwards. She slowly got up from her place on the grass, smoothing her dress with her hands. She rolled her eyes and sighed angrily as she noticed the large grass stains on her freshly white dress. I felt the guilt creep up again, noticing how good she looked in that dress, even with her makeup all smudged and her curls fading into straight strands. She did all of this for me, and I showed up like some drunk asshole. "I'm sorry," I whispered again, finally looking up at her. I had to put a hand over my eyes, to shield them from the bright sun she was standing in front of.

She seemed like she already put up the emotional wall I knew so well and I instantly regretted even taking that first sip last night. "It's fine, honestly," she said, shaking her head. She primped at her curls and looked anywhere but at me. "What did I say last night?" I asked, suddenly curious. It obviously affected her, because she couldn't even look me in the eyes anymore. I thought we were making progress from all of that bullshit. She shrugged her shoulders. "Some babble on how you didn't even drink. Then you told me about your..." she faded off and I sat up fully. What did I tell her? "Told you about my what?"

"Your Dad," she finished, mumbling. My eyes bulged and I winced, not liking what that just did to the headache currently going on. I shook my head, throwing it in my hands. I angrily ran my hands through my hair and pulled the ends. I never told anyone about that. Trust me to tell a complete stranger my whole life story after a couple of shots. "What did I tell you about...him?" I asked, anxious to see how much I actually did tell her. She had her head down and was putting a piece of hair behind her ear. She shifted her bare feet in the green blades beneath her. "How you want him back..." she continued.

I froze instantly. No I didn't. "I did?" my voice squeaked as I spoke. The only person I talked to about that was my Mom. And I barely even told her anything. She only nodded her head. Finally looking up at me, I noticed her face held that stupid pity look to it. I shook my head at her and put my hands up. "No, not that look," I spat, venom seeping from my voice. "I get enough of that shit from everyone else I know. Don't do that." "I'm sorry. I just didn't know that that's why you wouldn't talk about-" I cut her off immediately. I wasn't about to talk to her about all of this. As much as I felt that sense of comfort whenever I was around her, she didn't even know my middle name from God's sakes. I wasn't about to tell her my whole life story on how much I missed my Dad.

"Stop!" I yelled. She winced in fear from my shift in tone, but I couldn't feel bad right now. Not with that look she just gave me, and the prying that I knew was about to come. "Evan, I didn't mean..." "No, it's fine. Just don't ask me about it, okay? Forget all of the shit I told you last night. I was drunk. Doesn't mean any of it was true!" I spat, getting up from my position on the floor. I brushed my butt off, and didn't even make eye contact with her as I made my way around the building. I felt a tug on my arm when I heard, "Evan!"

"What!" I yelled, spinning around to face a guilty looking Bailey. I felt my heart squeeze a little bit for her, but I didn't let it affect me this time. I don't make exceptions for anyone. Especially people I don't know. "Leslie's number," she said, her voice quiet. "You asked me for it last night. Here," she said, handing me a tiny slip of paper with numbers scrawled onto it. I snatched it from her trembling hand and stomped off to my car. As I turned the key, starting it up, I gripped the steering wheel tightly, my fists turning white from the contact. I was more pissed off at myself than I was at Bailey. I did the stupidest shit when I was drunk, and always regretted anything I said or did the next morning. Why in the hell would I tell some random girl how much I miss my Dad? Why would I spill stuff like that to someone I didn't even know? And the biggest question on my mind was, why did she care so much?

"Fuck Dad, do you see the kind of shit you get me into?" I shouted up at the blue sky above me. I was locking up my car and walking to Aaron's door. I knocked lightly and he immediately pulled it open. Trust Aaron to be wide awake at nine in the morning. "Hi," I snapped; moving around him and into his house like it was my own. "Well hello to you too, sunshine," he said, humor in his voice. "Haha," I said sarcastically. I sat myself down on the stool in front of his counter, which he used as a dining table. I crossed my arms in front of me, shaking my head. I was trying to calm myself down, but nothing I was doing was working. I wanted to know how much I told the stupid girl in the first place.

"Let it out," he said, ushering me with his hand. He stood on the opposite side of the protruding counter. He leaned his elbows on the table and waited patiently for me to speak. "I got drunk last night," I started, clenching my fists. "What else is new?" he grinned, playfully. I really wasn't in the mood for humor today. "Shut up," I spewed. "I was supposed to be hanging out with some girl and I showed up drunk."

"What girl?" he asked, curiosity laced in his voice. "Some girl I met at that concert. Not the point," I said, waving my hand carelessly. "I told her about my Dad, dude." "And," he urged. What the hell did he mean, 'and'. "And I barely know this girl, Aar. Apparently I went on and on about how much I miss him and shit. I don't even tell my own mother about that crap, and I managed to tell her the biggest part of my life story," I said, throwing my hands up in the air. Aaron shook his head at me. "That obviously means something, Ev. You don't tell just anyone about your problems and you confided in her. That must mean you feel comfortable around her. What's the big deal?" he asked, shrugging his shoulders in a nonchalant way. I could wring his neck now, I swear. "What's the big deal?" I scoffed.

"The big deal is that I don't even know her!" I yelled, my voice rising as I continued. "She doesn't need to know my personal bullshit! She doesn't even know my middle name for God's sake, so why did she need to know about how I felt?!" I winced, the pain still pretty evident in my head from last night's drinking game I held with myself. "Aspirin?" Aaron asked. I nodded my head and he walked over to a cabinet high up. He took out two white colored pills and set it down in front of me. He walked over to his refrigerator, and took out two water bottles, setting one in front of me, next to them. As I took them, he continued with his rant.

"Look, Ev. Stop stressing over it, alright? What's there to worry about? You don't know everything you said right?" he questioned. I nodded my head and he continued again. "Well, who cares then?

You said so yourself, you barely know the girl. You probably won't ever see her again, if you really don't want to. So stop stressing out about it. You have enough to stress about as it is. You can't do anything about what just happened. Just move forward," he shrugged, taking a sip from the bottle in his hand.

I contemplated what he said over in my head and realized that like always, Aaron was right. If I really don't want to see her again, I don't have to. I didn't plan on going to the theatre, aside from seeing Leslie again, so who cares? I can just move on from this and find someone else to spend my time with. The only thing I could think of after that was the busty blonde from the bar that I knew all too well. After some messing around with his Xbox and eating most of the food he stocked in his kitchen, I left a couple of hours later, heading for home. I remembered that Bailey had given me Leslie's number and I decided it was time that I moved forward with something new in my life. Something I didn't need to be stressing over. Leslie seemed fun. And fun was something I definitely needed right now. I fished the number out of my pocket and pressed the Bluetooth button on my car's touch screen. After typing the number in my phone at a red light, I hit dial and waited for her to answer.

"Hello?" the small, but cheery blonde's voice rang through my car. I smiled. "Leslie? It's Evan, from the show last week. Listen, I feel guilty about running out on you in the middle of our conversation the other day. I was wondering if you wanted to go out to dinner with me. Maybe...tomorrow night?" I asked, already knowing what her answer would be. I heard her giggle softly over the receiver and she quickly answered with a peppy, "Of course!" I bid her a goodbye and kept a grin on my face as I drove home. I kissed my

Mom on the head and rubbed little Greg's head as I made my way home, completely bypassing any questions as to where and who I was with last night.

It was a couple of hours before I had to be out with Leslie that I noticed little Greg had gotten salsa stained onto my one and only nice looking tie and I knew I was screwed. I had about two hours to kill before I had to pick her up, so I decided that I could give it a shot by running to the mall really quick and picking one up. I grabbed my keys and headed down the road, still quite happy at how things were going. I was going on a date with a hot girl, who seemed to be a stress reliever instead of causer. It was definitely something new compared to the dramatic bullshit I've been going through these past few weeks. I haven't seen one of those in years.

As I made it into the parking lot, I was looking for a space to park when I almost froze at the song that came on the radio. It was the Baby Blue Eyes song from Phil Keys and my mind suddenly flashed to the night on the rooftop with Bailey Keys herself. I replayed the moment I asked her about the song, and my mind went back to the memory of her bright hazel eyes when they looked up at me as I asked her questions.

I suddenly felt bad for how I treated her. I didn't care in the moment when I yelled at her because I was only thinking about myself and how much of an ass I can be when I drink too much. I didn't care how she felt then, but I kind of did now. I didn't think I would ever see her again to apologize, but I found myself wishing that I could see her again. What was with me anymore? I was going on a date in almost two hours with a hot girl who didn't resemble anything close to Bailey. So why did my mind keep running back to her all the time? I clicked my car key's button to lock up and made my way to the mall entrance, heading straight for the men's department in the closest store I could find. I didn't have time to run around aimlessly without leaving Leslie waiting.

I rushed over to the tie collection that they had and picked up a navy blue one that wasn't too proper looking, but matched with my shirt. I didn't bother looking through the prices, just made my way up to the cashier. I looked around the store while I waited in line and stopped dead when the familiar light red hair caught my eyes. No fucking way. Not this again. "Bailey?" I asked, slowly. I didn't know how she would react to seeing me again. She turned around quickly at the mention of her name and her eyes widened like they did yesterday morning. I felt incredibly awkward, knowing how I treated her. She merely waved at me. I didn't even hear a peep from her as she turned back around and faced front, waiting to be attended to. I suddenly felt a surge of confidence go through me and got out of line, making a bee line for her.

I knew I only had about an hour and half before meeting Leslie, and I knew the lines were extremely long. I didn't care. I just wanted to make things right. "Look, I'm sorry," I whispered, touching her arm slightly to get her attention. She jumped, not realizing how close I had gotten. "I just don't do that kind of shit, sober," I said, lowering my voice. Some bald headed man with a tiny stature kept glaring at me like I was going to butt in front of him in line. I raised an eyebrow at him, but shook my head, remembering what I was doing. "It's okay," she whispered back, not looking at me. "It's obviously not, because you won't even look at me," I joked, smiling a little. I was hoping I could get something out of her to show that I was sorry and that she forgave me. She finally made eye contact, but her facial appearance showed nothing close to happy or forgiveness.

"Look, why do you even care?" she snapped. "Because I feel really guilty for how I acted yesterday and I'm sorry," I mumbled. "So you say sorry for being a total ass, not one but two days in a row and I'm just supposed to forgive you?" she whisper-yelled, sending me death glares. "Two days in a row?" I questioned.

"Yeah, showing up drunk after asking someone out doesn't exactly read nicest man on earth, does it?" she said, crossing her arms. I sighed. I kept her gaze as I continued. "Look, I'm sorry. I can't change how everything happened, but all I want to know is if you can forgive me and maybe we could...be friends at least?" I asked, anxious as to what she would say. She eyed me for what felt like ages, her expression softening just a bit. "Fine. Friends. Just stop being an asshole every time someone wants to actually talk to you," she sighed. I grinned. "Friends it is."

Chapter 11

It had been about a month since I'd last gotten into a fight with Evan Tyler Warren. Yeah, his middle name's Tyler. He made sure that I knew his middle name before he told me anything else more personal relating to his life. He was weird. "Bail, I need a beer," he huffed. Evan slumped down into the tan, leather recliner in my living room, crossing his arms.

"Well now that you're twenty-one, go buy your own beer," I retorted, smiling lightly at him. Evan and I agreed a while ago that we would try to be friends. It was going well so far, considering he was such an asshole to me when we first met. The tiny jabs at me became far less frequent if I didn't question any further into his personal life. The fewer questions asked, the easier we got along. It became a daily thing, and I didn't try to provoke him. I just wanted to be friends with him, and I didn't want to ruin the friendship we were beginning to have. If it meant not knowing about his Dad, then I could deal with that.

I didn't quite like the arrangement that we had, me staying quiet when something really personal came up, but I learned to deal with it. It was who Evan was. He didn't like to let people in, and I was really the only one who understood what that was like. I didn't let anyone in at all, let alone Evan and I wasn't about to. I knew what it was like to keep to a secret from someone. I knew what it was like to build walls to keep people out. I wasn't about to be a hypocrite and question why he was doing the same to me, no matter how close we got. Evan and I had a stable friendship, just not a really close one. And I could deal with that.

I wanted to keep Evan around. He was kind of like my safety blanket, the one I could always count on to be there if I really need to let everything out. I didn't know when that moment would come, but I knew I would crack one day, and I had a feeling he would be there to comfort me if I needed it. As long as Leslie didn't mind. Oh yes, he's dating Leslie Burkhart.

They started dating around the same time Evan and I became friends, and let's just say neither her nor I were too fond of the other. We got along as much as we needed to at work, until she found out that Evan was my close friend, and I found out she was his girlfriend. It was like two opposites trying to get along, but never working. Leslie was the blonde, free-spirited partier, where as I was the quiet, unsociable red-head with a million and one secrets. She wasn't someone I considered a friend, and I'm pretty sure I could say the same for her. Work suddenly became extremely awkward and not entertaining. When I would ask questions, she would give me the bitchiest attitude imaginable. If she saw me talking to an attendee at a concert, she would give me death glares when I wasn't looking.

When I walked into work with Evan...well let's just say all hell would break loose. I wouldn't mind so much if she didn't have such a reputation as a slut around this town. She'd been rumored to be sleeping with as many as twenty different guys, all in the course of a few months. Most were attendees from indie rock shows at the theatre. Others would remain unnamed and unseen. Evan didn't deserve a skanky girlfriend, and she sure as hell didn't deserve a guy like him.

"Shut up," he joked, sticking his tongue out at me like a little boy. That was one of the few quirks that I enjoyed about him, how boyish he could be in some moments. "You want me to go get it for you because you're too lazy, but you must have forgotten that I'm under aged. And you're a boarder-line alcoholic," I stuck my tongue out back at him. "Whatever," he scoffed, playfully. "And I am not a boarder-line alcoholic," he said, crossing his arms across his chest, eyeing me down. "Whatever you say, Ev," I giggled. "So where are your parents?" he asked quietly, like he was waiting for a reaction that leaded to a blow up. When curiosity came into the picture, one of us would ease into the question, just in case it became too much to talk about. I rolled my eyes, not caring about this question.

"Dad's off laying down vocals for a new song and my mother is out shopping with her friends," I said, waving my hand nonchalantly. He merely nodded his head and flicked between television stations on the flat screen aimlessly. As I was flipping through a magazine, enjoying the comfortable quiet filling the room, he cleared his throat. I looked up and met his eyes. "Listen," he said, suddenly making the air in the room serious. "My mom's having a 'guest' over tonight," he went on, making air quotes. "And I kind of need a scapegoat for later..." he faded out. My eyes widened slightly. This was the first piece of personal information I saw from Evan since the night he confessed to me back at the field. He noticed my silence and continued to ramble on. "But, you don't have to come if you don't want to! I mean I definitely wouldn't want to come to an uncomfortable family dinner with someone else. Especially with this new..." "Sure," I quickly nodded, cutting him from his rant. This should be interesting.

When I sat at Evan's dining room table with his mother, little brother and her 'guest' Chief Williams from the firehouse, I found myself feeling really uncomfortable. Usually, when I was invited over for dinner, the conversation was easy-going, enjoyable and full of jokes. Tonight's dinner was the furthest thing from that. It was so quiet that you could only hear the sound of metal forks scrapping against glass plates, and Chief Williams loudly chewing at his steak. I saw Evan cringe, just watching him eat it. It was quite gross, in my opinion, because I was always taught to eat with my mouth closed, not like a cow. "So," Mrs. Warren sighed. "How was everyone's day?" She looked around at the bored facial expressions of everyone around the table, except for Greg's. He looked so anxious as he awaited someone to finally speak up so he could talk.

He looked like he was trying hard to imitate his older brother though, staying silent and brooding. "Mommy, today in school, I drew a picture of a fire-truck and wrote about what I wanted to be when I grow up, and I got an A plus and a sticker from Ms.Amdel for it!" he cheered, smiling up at everyone. I smiled back at him, nodding my head in approval. Chief Williams, for the first time tonight, spoke up. "Good job, son," he grinned, wiping his mouth with the back of his hand. I was silently thanking Evan for making me sit next to him, and not next to the disgusting being on the other side. Evan froze. His hand, which was holding a forkful of mashed potatoes, dangled in midair and then he dropped it onto his plate. "He's not your son, Cal," he snapped, giving him a death glare.

"Now Evan, I'm pretty sure that's not what he-" He cut off his mom and got up from the chair next to me. He threw his napkin down and glared at Williams. "He's Gregory Warren's son," he spat, finally walking out of the room. I heard the front door slam shut a few seconds afterwards and the awkwardness set in. "I'm sorry," I said to his mom, getting up from my chair. Even though I didn't agree with his savage eating habits, I threw Cal an apologetic look and made my way outside to Evan. I shut the door lightly behind me, and padded out into the dark night, searching for his figure with the little light coming from the porch wall lamp. I found him perched against his car, throwing little rocks at Chief Williams's car.

I ran over to him and hit his arm. "Stop that." "No," he exclaimed, like it was not a big deal. He continued messing up Cal's car with little dents in his shiny, new topless red Mustang. Fed up with his childish actions, I hit his arm harder and the fistful of rocks he once held onto were now splashed all over the gravel beneath us. "Hey!" he yelled at me. He threw me a glare and I quietly ignored it.

"No, that's not right, Evan. You may be mad at him but you can't dent up his brand new car that obviously looked like it cost him a fortune." "Really? Watch me," he threatened, bending down to pick up the rocks again. I grabbed him by the back of his tight-fitted ivory t-shirt and pulled him back up sharply. "Stop it, Evan!" I warned. He got back up and shouted. "God!" before sinking against his car and onto the ground on his bum. He was such a child sometimes. I sunk down next to him and took his larger hand in mine. I ignored the slight tingling sensation I felt shoot through my own and looked up at my friend with concern. "What's wrong?"

I questioned, keeping my eyes on him. He didn't look up at me, but stayed staring at the black gravel. "Everything's such shit," he said, throwing a rock against the adjacent garage in front of us. "That's not his fucking son." "That's not what he meant, Evan and you know it. Now what's really bugging you about this guy?" "He's not going to replace my father, Bailey!" he yelled, finally looking up at me with those beautiful grassy colored eyes. I kept his gaze, waiting for him to continue.

"I know he's not just a 'guest'. He's my mom's date!" With the word 'date', he threw another rock at the garage, putting a small silver dent into the freshly painted white door. "Why can't your Mom date?" I questioned. He hadn't told me how long it had been since his Dad died, or how his Mom felt about the entire thing now. I only knew as much as he told me the night at the field, and I didn't want to stop questioning him anymore. He can't get mad at me just because I'm clueless. "Fate's an asshole!" he yelled, repeating my words from that same night. "My Dad's supposed to be the one here. NotCal," he gritted his teeth when he mentioned the chief's name.

I felt him grip my hand, silently showing me how much this was all eating away at his heart. I knew he wanted to tell me what happened, and I so badly wanted to know. I wanted to know what hurt this beautiful boy and why he was so sad sometimes. I wanted to make it all go away. I knew how it all felt to want to push people away, but I felt like I didn't want to be pushed anymore. "Evan," I prodded, slowly. "How did your Dad..." I found myself fading off and feeling anxious as to what he would say.

The major part of me was expecting him to bounce up and start yelling at me, just like he did a month ago when I prodded too much. I saw him heave a huge breath and put a death grip on my palm. I gripped it back, letting him know that he could tell me. "He died during 9/11," he stated, keeping firm eye contact with the ground. At that moment, I felt my heart break into tiny, microscopic pieces. I felt sadness and guilt flutter in my stomach and tears ready to prick my eyes, just knowing how he must be feeling. "Evan, I'm so sorry," I whispered, keeping the tight grip on his hand.

"And the shittiest part is, I didn't even get to say goodbye to him," he breathed, his voice sounding choked. I felt the pain for him eat away at me, just seeing how it broke him. "Oh Evan," I sighed, resting my head on his shoulder. I gripped his hand, using the other to rub it affectionately. "That's why you can't ever talk about it," I continued. He merely nodded, not wanting to go any further. I had so many more questions to ask him, like what happened that day. I wanted to know why he felt like he was such a shitty person. I had so many questions, but I knew that he didn't want to go on anymore, and I wasn't about to make him.

"Lanie died too," I spit out, slowly. I wasn't expecting to tell Evan this news on this night, at this specific time. I really wasn't expecting to tell him at all honestly. I just felt like he needed to know that I knew what the pain felt like. That he needed to know that he wasn't alone. "What?" he choked, finally looking up at me. He ran a hand underneath his runny nose, and pushed his hand through his hair.

I lifted my head up off of his shoulder and nodded my head. I pushed a piece of hair behind my ear and looked down at the ground. Now it was my turn to not make eye contact. "How did she..." he breathed, still holding onto my hand. "Brain cancer," I said, feeling the tears well up at my lids. I hadn't cried in front of anyone in so long. I didn't want to do it now, no matter how close I felt to Evan. I furiously wiped underneath my lids, hating the traitor tears that fell and the way I could feel my heart re-breaking again when I spoke about her. "Bailey, I'm so sorry," he mimicked my earlier words, gripping my hand more tightly as he spoke. "I just thought..." I breathed, running a hand over my stray hairs to get them out of my eyes. "That I wanted you to know that I know the feeling," I finished, taking a deep breath. "God," he sighed. I finally got the courage to look up at him and noticed he was staring up at the sky again.

"Why do our lives suck so much?" he laughed. It was small, and sounded choked up from the mess of emotions playing around about us, but he laughed all the same. I felt my heart swell at the sound, and felt a little piece of sadness slide away just hearing it. It was amazing how much of an affect another person can have on you. "I don't know," I sighed, looking up at the golden, tiny stars with him. "You know," I continued, taking in another shaky, heavy breath. "Lanie used to do this all the time." "What? Spill her confessions on a dirty gravel driveway?" he smirked at me.

I shook my head, smiling slightly at him too. "No. She used to look up at the stars all the time. She said it made her feel better no matter how bad she was feeling. Lanie said you could look up at the stars and know that you weren't alone. That someone else out there was feeling the same way you were." He tightened his hold on my hand again and whispered, "You're not alone, Bail." I looked down at him and felt my heart skip a beat at the way his green eyes stared into mine. It was like we were sharing the same pain, the same sadness, but the same memories as well. We didn't need words, or big gestures. We just needed to grip the other's hand and know that we weren't alone. That we had each other.

I felt the air around us get a little chillier, but neither one of us had left the other's sight. I so badly wanted to lean in and place my lips on his, no matter how bad it would make me look. I didn't care that he had a girlfriend. I didn't care that he might not feel the same way. I just knew that I've been feeling this intense pull since we first met on the rooftop and I hadn't shaken it since.

I could have sworn I saw him lean in slightly, keeping eye contact with me. I noticed his eyes turn softer than I had ever seen them, and an emotion I have yet to see bubbled beneath the surface. This was all brand new. Just as I was about to do the same, to meet him in the bliss of the middle ground, I jumped at the sound of his phone going off. He jumped back slightly too, clearing his throat heartily. I watched as he pulled his iPhone out of his back pocket and he widened his eyes. "It's Les," he stated, looking up at me. I didn't know what to think. I didn't even know what to say. I felt my mouth open, not knowing what was going to come out.

He stared at me, hopefully, waiting for my reaction. It's like he wanted to ask for my permission to answer her call or not. I didn't know what to do or what to say. I could only sit there, gaping like a stupid fish as he looked back at the ringing phone. "I'd better take this," he said, quickly, getting up from the ground. He brushed the gravel off of his bum and put the phone to his ear. "Hey babe," I heard him say as he walked back into the house. His voice wasn't cheery. It was gruff, but not in a blatant way like he had been hiding something. It was like it was so natural to ease right into a conversation with her. Just at the mention of the word 'babe', and I felt my heart re-breaking for the third time that night. Why couldn't he call me 'babe'?

Chapter 12

I haven't talked to Bailey since the night that I told her about my Dad. I was too much of a coward to even face her at this point. I don't know why I said the things that I said. I don't know I did the things that I did. It was one of those moments where you're completely irrational and just let it all out. It felt like I was holding so many things in that I couldn't take it anymore. And it I could let it out to anyone at that moment, it was Bailey. How do you look someone in the eyes when you bared your soul to them, and almost kissed them right in your driveway? I sure as hell couldn't do it.

I had a girlfriend, and a very hot one at that. Leslie was fun, she made me laugh, smile and even listened to me when I needed her. I had told Leslie that my Dad had died, but I never told her how or when, or any of the nasty details. I just felt like she needed to know when my birthday party came up and my Dad hadn't called to wish me a happy 21st. She was surprised to say the least. She was surprised that I didn't tell her. I didn't know why she was. Death was not something that you just blurted out in the middle of a dinner conversation. You didn't nonchalantly bypass it during a phone call. It wasn't something sufferers could talk about easily.

And when you take it the hardest, like I do, you didn't want to tell anyone at all, no matter the conversation.

She wanted to know more, every time a deep conversation ensued, but I would always drive the conversation in a different direction, letting the topic fade into the background of her brain. She was slightly air-headed so that part wasn't so hard to do. Even though she was pretty hard to talk to intellectually, she was still someone I could have fun with. I needed to have fun, because I was tired of being some depressed asshole who didn't smile anymore. And Leslie made me smile. But Bailey, on the other hand, was a completely different story. Bailey made me laugh, made me smile, made me angry, sad, confused, and frustrated. But I wouldn't trade the girl for the world. I counted her as a close friend, even though she didn't feel that we were. I didn't want to open up to her. Especially after everything she heard the night at the field. Ever since we made up, we never spoke about that night. I never prodded more answers from her on what she heard, and she never prodded more into my personal life. We went on with the friendship like that night had never happened, and I planned on keeping it that way before anything else became like a Dr. Phil rerun.

Never asking personal questions was like an unspoken rule between us that no one would ever understand. I knew she was hiding things from me that she didn't want me to know; just like she knew I was hiding things about my life as well. We didn't prod because we knew how the other would get. As much as I wanted to know what was going on in her life, especially when the awkwardness set in during the minimal moments of her parents being home when I was there, I didn't push. Merely because I didn't want to be pushed myself. I always looked at it like, you get as much as you give. I wanted to know Bailey so much more than what I already knew about her, but I just wasn't ready to bare my feelings about my Dad to her like we were siblings or close family. I didn't work that way. But, when Cal pissed me off so much that I wanted to wring his neck for even stepping foot in my house, I felt like I needed to finally come out with it. She didn't understand that why after so long, I cared so much that my Mom was clearly dating again.

She deserved love as much as the next person. I didn't want her to wait around forever, like Dad was actually going to show up at the doorstep again or something. I knew that she was lonely and needed a man for herself, but I wasn't ready to accept that. You'd think that after almost eleven years, acceptance paved a way for you, but not for me. I wanted to punch Cal in his cow chewing, spit slapping mouth for even referring to little Greg as his son. I knew deep down that that's not what his intentions were, but everything seemed to be unraveling at the seams that night, and I couldn't take it anymore. When Bailey came out and silently willed me to let her in, I felt like I didn't have a choice anymore. I was giving into the pull that had attracted me to her since the night from the rooftop. I was finally letting someone see the pain and angst I was living with day by day, and she actually knew how it felt.

I wasn't expecting her to suddenly blurt out that her sister died. I didn't have the slightest clue that she was holding something in that was that deep. But I felt a small weight being lifted off of my shoulders knowing that someone finally knew how it felt. I wasn't being fed bullshit advice or excuses from people who pretended anymore. I was actually letting someone in who knew the pain that my heart felt since the day that my Dad walked into that burning building. But, I also felt a piece of heart break knowing that she was going through something so deep, and no one even knew.

It was weird how I felt so drawn to this girl, but dating a girl like Les. Don't get me wrong, I really liked Leslie. She was something I needed in a time when I was so down I couldn't function properly anymore. But Bailey pulled me in so much, that I didn't know if I could pull myself back anymore. We were like stretched out rubber bands. The more we pulled away, the more the rubber was about to break. We wanted to desperately to retract and come back in. Or, at least that's how I saw it. I had no idea how she felt. All I knew was that I wanted to kiss her so badly that night. I knew I had a girlfriend waiting by the phone for me. I knew we were getting so close as friends that I could screw everything up. I knew that I was even oblivious to how she felt. But I didn't care. I was tired of pulling at the rubber.

I wanted to finally let go. But when Leslie called, I didn't know how to react anymore. It was like the view of her name on my phone screen was a bucket of cold ice water being dropped on top of me. I realized everything I would be giving up, and I realized the risks I would be taking jumping into something like that. When did I become such a pansy ass like this? I knew Bailey was probably waiting for me to call. Today was the morning of our usual breakfast get together at the Opium Diner near her house. We joked while we ate pancakes, and ate off of each other's plates without a care in the world about our personal lives getting in the way.

I actually really liked those mornings, because it felt like a getaway from all of the shit in my life. But I didn't think I could go through with that today, especially after ignoring her for days since the night in the driveway. I decided I would call Leslie, because she was the second distraction on my list, and I really needed one today. We decided to meet for lunch at this stupid little posh restaurant that she loved so much. In my opinion, it was ugly with its blood red walls, and shit colored leather booths. But, you take what you can get. We made our way to the shit colored booth a few hours later, while my stomach grumbled to get my attention. Leslie was wearing a soft yellow cashmere sweater with some skinny jeans, trying to look nice in front of her unknown peers at the rich restaurant.

I, on the other hand, went for the casual look, with a dark grey t-shirt and some jeans, added with some messed up Converse sneakers. I honestly could care less what the rich snobs in this place thought of me. All I cared about was getting some food in my noisy stomach and getting rid of the mess in my head. A girl like Bailey could do that to you. "Hi, my name's Bailey. I'll be your server today. What can I get you?" a too familiar voice asked next to me. My eyes shot up to her and they almost fell out their sockets. I swallowed loudly and placed my menu down in front of me. Leslie, on the opposite side of the table, looked up and glared at Bailey, showing her disgust. I didn't even want to get in the middle of this cat fight right now. I just wanted to hide my face in shame and peel out of here in my car.

"Um," she gulped, only looking at me for a second, before looking down at her pad of paper in her hand. "Drinks?" "I'll have an ice water with lemon, of course," she sneered, throwing a piece of blonde, pin straight hair over her shoulder. Bailey only nodded her head, writing down Leslie's order. I cleared my throat, trying not to gap at her like an idiot. Before I could find words to form, Les spoke for me. "He'll have a Pepsi, extra ice," she smiled up at Bailey, clearly showing that she was the girlfriend who knew everything I wanted. She was obviously the better girl here because she could order for me, and act like a girlfriend, and Bailey couldn't. In her mind, she was winning this fight. A fight that I didn't even want to be included in. "Be right back," she breathed, not ever meeting my eyes. I rubbed my hands together, trying to get a hold of myself. This was Bailey we're talking about here. We were such good friends before all of this stupid confessing and physical shit got in the way. Why could you never stay friends with a girl for long?

Either you or her always felt something in the long run. It was inevitable. I had fallen below the trap with no going back. But deep down, I knew that this was my trap from the get go. But, I just needed her back as my friend. I didn't need all of the other shit if she didn't want it. Like always, I manage to screw everything up. We couldn't part ways now. I confessed to her, and I knew I would probably crack later on. I needed her to be there when I did. I damn well couldn't confide in Leslie. She'd coddle me like a five year old. When Bailey came back with our drinks, I had words prepared and confidence somewhat ready. She placed our cups down, placing the straws in the middle. I decided now was my time to speak up.

"Since when did you work here?" I questioned, looking up at her. "I thought you took a job at the theatre." She stopped dead, slowly moving her eyes towards mine. I was guessing that she wasn't expecting me to say anything to her. I hadn't said a word in almost two weeks. "I uh...needed the second job. Needed to get out of the house," she shrugged, going back to her pad of paper. "Must suck being poor," Leslie scoffed, smiling sweetly up at Bailey. I shook my head, running my hands through my hair. If she only knew who Bailey's dad was. And she couldn't refrain from a cat fight for more than a minute.

Bailey sent her a glare before asking what he wanted for lunch. Leslie ordered a Caesar salad, dressing on the side. I ordered a bacon cheeseburger with extra fries awkwardly without making any eye contact. She nodded her head quickly before speeding off into the kitchen to give the orders. I stared into the direction she went, wondering what the hell to do. Granted, as much as this awkwardness was uncomfortable for me, I couldn't shake the pull I still felt towards her. I wanted her back for my distraction. I wanted her back to joke around with, to argue with, to drink with, to laugh with, and to confide in. I couldn't do that with just anyone anymore, and Bailey was all I had. I was tired of this bullshit I kept doing to myself and decided that I needed to take a stand. I stood up quickly from the booth and threw down my napkin.

As I walked in the direction Bailey went, I heard Leslie scream my name. "Evan, where the hell are you going?" I ignored her and burst through the black swinging door, facing a bunch of kitchen staff with stunned expressions. I wasn't allowed back here, that much was clear, and they were mostly expecting another waiter. When it was obvious that I wasn't dressed in black like a waiter should be, I was met with screams and hushed tones. "Sir, you can't be back here," a woman who looked to be in her late thirties came towards me, trying to usher me back the way I came. I tugged my arm out of her grasp. She seemed frightened of me as I glared at her.

”Tall red head, about this high,” I gestured with a hand to around my chest at the woman, trying to show her how tall Bailey was. "Where did she go?” I asked, frustration clear in my voice. ”That way,” she whimpered, pointing a long, bony finger to my right, through a set of back doors, leading outside. I guess I was pretty intimidating when I was angry. I stormed through the door, confidence radiating from me. I didn't even know where that feeling came from.

She was sitting on a milk crate, her head in her hands when I burst through. Her head shot up at the sound and she seemed startled. ”Evan?” she said, standing up quickly. "Why are you back here?””Because I can't stand these stupid games we play with each other anymore!” I shouted, throwing my hands up in the air. She stared at me, wide eyed and somewhat angry.“Games?” she scoffed. "Want to talk about games, Evan?” she threatened. I crossed my arms, waiting for her to go on. ”You're the fucking mastermind at it!” she yelled. It was the first time I heard her use the F word in a sentence and I was somewhat shocked.

”First, you give me shit for not letting you in. Then you ask me out,” she counted off examples on each finger angrily. "You show up like a drunken asshole and spew shit about your Dad. Then when I question you, you scream at me like some kind of animal for wanting to help you out!” I was shaking by this point. She was pointing out my flaws, making it clear that I was fuck up, and I wasn't having it anymore. I can blame myself for things all I wanted to. I could say I was a fuck up as long as I wanted. But she couldn't sit there and blame me for things she'd done too. ”Oh really? I get mad when someone questions me? How about you, huh?” I said, pointing a hard finger in her direction.

"You're being such a fucking hypocrite, Bailey! You hide things from me all the damn time. You haven't even told me what the tattoo means! You don't let me know about your parents! Hell, two weeks ago was the first time you even remotely let me in to begin with!" She glared at me. If looks could kill, I'd be on the ground right about now. She stalked up to me and got close to my face. "How dare you," she seethed, looking straight into my eyes. "You keep everything from me, Evan!" her voice was rising by the minute. She backed away a little, throwing her hands up in the air.

"You never ever let me know anything going on in your life! Hell, I only heard your friend Aaron's name in passing, ONE time! You find out you mistakenly tell me about your Dad, and you freak out like you just spilled a government secret! Talk about being a god damn hypocrite, Evan!" "Bailey, you don't know shit! Who do you think you are?!" I yelled. I could feel my face heating up from the exertion and my breathing was becoming heavy. So much for fixing things. She wanted a fight; I would give her a god damn fight. "Who do I think I am?" she breathed, angrily, pointing at herself.

"I'm sorry; I was under the impression that we were friends Evan! Or as you put it, best friends!" "What's your point? Because I say we're friends, it suddenly gives you access to everything going on in my life?!" "Well it sure as hell gives me access to hear something other than the weather and your dirty jokes Ev!" she said, throwing her hands up again. Her cheeks were tinted pink and she took a deep breath, steadying herself. When she calmed down, she whispered, "Why won't you let me in?" "Because you scare the shit out of me, okay?!" I yelled, running my hands through my hair in frustration.

There was no going back now, and I didn't think I could stop if I wanted to. "And you don't think you scare the shit out of me?" she yelled back at me. She didn't need an explanation, she knew, like always, what I was talking about. "I never tell people anything that goes in my life! Only Aaron, and he's a somewhat exception because he knew who my Dad was! You, you're just some girl who I met at a concert while I was somewhat drunk!" I yelled, watching as her face fell a little at my words.

"And for some fucking reason, I feel the need to share so many things with you and tell you how I feel. I feel like no one gets it like you do, and I don't feel this good around anyone else but you. And it scares the hell out of me, Bailey!" I turned to the side, slightly, breathing heavily. I ran my hands through the spiked up mess placed on top of my head and realized what I needed to do. "Oh hell," I stated before grabbing her by the waist and pushing her up against the brick wall. She went to open her mouth to come back at me, I suppose. Before she could, I roughly pressed my lips to hers and kissed her like my life depended on it.

Chapter 13

I was shocked to a stand still when Evan placed his lips on mine. I didn't kiss him back at first, because I still trying to figure out what just happened. But when I finally realized what was going on, I slowly wrapped my arms around his neck as he laced his around my middle. I moaned as he asked for access with his tongue. I quickly granted him access, and kissed him like I didn't want to let go. From the tight grip around my waist, I was thinking that he didn't want to let go either. I played with the wisps of black hair at his neck, and when I pulled on it slightly, he moaned into my mouth.

I smiled into the kiss, loving what I could do to him. I'd been waiting for this moment since we met, and it was better than I could have ever pictured it to be. Of course, my first picture was of us in the field, but because of certain events, that never happened. But I was far more than happy to have it happening, right here, and right now. I was pushed up against the bricks, with Evan's hands sliding up and down my sides, and it felt like pure bliss. The way our lips formed together made my heart almost swell at the thought. I don't think I've ever had a kiss like this before. And I was hoping this wasn't our last.

As he pulled out, he bit my lip slightly, and I whimpered at the contact. The tiny pain turned into pleasure and I wanted to melt right in the spot I was standing. If he hadn't been holding me by my waist, my knees would have bucked beneath me. He raised a large hand to my hair and pushed a strand behind my ear. My eyes were still closed and he pressed our foreheads together. I could feel his minty breath mingling with mine as we took in the air we needed after a kiss like that.

He sounded just about as out of breath as I was, so I was hoping that this meant a whole lot for him too. When he confessed to me how he felt, I could have recited the words back to him like they were written down in front of me. The fact that I wasn't the only one who felt so drawn to a stranger in the beginning made me feel much less like an idiot, and more like a person who was falling for someone else.

I felt tingles in the warm place where his hand was still placed on my hip and smiled at the thought. I opened my eyes and was met with his grassy, bright ones. He was smiling at me too, and it was the first real smile I'd seen him show since the night that I met him on the rooftop.

"You felt it too?" I breathed. He only nodded in agreement, the smile still playing on his lips. "I'm glad I'm not the only one who-" He cut me off saying 'Sh', before leaning in and kissing the life out of me again. Oh yeah, I could definitely get used to this.

Later on, when my shift was over and Evan had left Leslie secretly at the restaurant, I was nestling against the most perfect boy, in the familiar grassy field behind the theatre. After nine at night, the back door was locked up so drunks and idiots couldn't come back to the employee section, so no one ever came back here.

I was slightly worried about Leslie's words that I eavesdropped on in the earlier fight between her and Evan. She obviously didn't want to break up, and it seemed like Evan didn't know how to say it was over. Leslie Burkhart doesn't go down without a fight, and she threatened that she would be back eventually.

She would be back to win Evan's heart if it was the last thing she did. A bit overdramatic in my opinion, considering they only dated for a month. But, that was Leslie. She would go into hysterics if the drug store ran out of her favorite shampoo. Everything was a fight, and she would always win. At the end of the argument, they left things sort of in unsettled territory. He never actually said he wanted to break up with her, just that he needed some time to think things over. She said that she didn't understand what the hell he needed time for, but if it's what he wanted, she'd gladly give it to him.

Normally, I don't like being the 'other woman' in a situation like this, but my feelings for Evan have been held back for so long. Now that they were out in the open, I couldn't just sit back and let Leslie take it all for the win this time. I needed to fight back, and finally get what I deserved. I wasn't about to let a guy like Evan go. But for now, I was just letting everything get pushed to the side. I would deal with it all at a later time. For now, I was just hoping that this time she wouldn't actually win.

There was a soft sound of basses thumping behind us in the building from the show going on, but neither one of us seemed to notice. He was playing with my hair, pushing it away from my eyes, and I was quietly relishing in the feeling of being in his arms when I needed it the most. My parents were away on vacation, and I was certainly not a mere thought in their pretty heads, so I could stay this way as long as I wanted to. I ran my hand along his chest, feeling the curves of his muscles beneath his thin, grey shirt.

He stopped my hand from walking across his chest and held it up slightly, so he could see while lying down. It was the hand with the infinity tattoo and he was eyeing it closely. He ran his finger over the tattoo like he did the night when he played with the bottle on the roof; like he was off in his own head space again.

"Tell me what you're thinking," I prodded, my voice small. I let him run his finger over as many times as he wanted to, tracing the lines with the tip of his pointer finger. "Why did you get this specific tattoo?" he asked, his voice gruff from lying down. I hadn't taken my head off of his chest, so I kept my gaze on his finger while he traced. I tried to ignore the tingles his skin left on mine every time he touched me. I breathed in a heavy breath and finally let it out, knowing I could trust him this time. We knew why the other was scared to say how they felt. We knew why we felt like we couldn't trust each other with our deepest fears and past memories. At this point, we knew we could confide in each other, now that we reached that common ground of understanding. "When we were kids, Lanie would always watch the Toy Story movies like it was a religion. She could practically recite every line each character said if you asked her to. Then one day, when she kept saying 'To infinity and beyond,' I was telling her I loved her before going off to a show with my Dad when I was about nine or so.

She said, with a huge smile on her face, 'You love me to infinity and beyond, right?'" I smiled at the memory. I took another breath before I went on. "And I said, 'Yup, to infinity and beyond.' It sort of became a thing after that. Whenever we would say we loved each other, she asked that question, and I would always say yes.

It was something no one else knew about but us, and something original, what no one else did. It was what was unique about us. So I took the most personal thing about her and put in a place that would always remind me of her." "Wow," I heard him breathe. I could practically hear the smile in his voice.

He was still absentmindedly tracing the tattoo while I continued. I figured there was no going back now. "It was the last thing we said to each other before she died," I breathed. "She was trying to make me stop crying and I had to leave to give her and her husband some privacy and I told her loved her. She of course said, 'To infinity and beyond, right?' and I said yes. It was the last thing I said to her before saying goodbye." I let out a shaky breath, and Evan did too. "That's a gift though," he stated. "How so?" I questioned. "You got to say goodbye before she left you for good. Not many people get to do that," he breathed.

"Are you saying that you didn't?" I prodded, sitting up a little to look at his face. He was staring up at the sky now, his fingers interlacing with mine in a somewhat tight grip. "I'm saying that," he sighed. "You should cherish that. That you got to say goodbye before she was taken from you." "But I'm asking if you got to say goodbye, Ev," I pushed. "Come on, I thought there was a somewhat silent agreement that we were done hiding our personal lives anymore." He sighed a bit angrily. "Do we have to do this right now, Bail?" he questioned. I rolled my eyes. "I just told you something I haven't told anyone before. And you think some other time would be better?" He huffed again before stating simply, "No, I didn't." He was still looking up at the stars above us. "He left for work that day and didn't come back."

"You didn't say goodbye before he left for work?" I questioned. I knew it wasn't the same thing as a goodbye when you know someone's permanently leaving, but I was still curious. "We got into a fight," he continued. "I got mad and he left for work. That was the last time I ever saw him," he breathed. "I'm so sorry Evan," I exclaimed, gripping his hand as I laid my head back down on his chest. Every time he told me about his past, I felt my heart break more and more for him.

"Want to know the best part?" he asked, sarcasm dripping in his tone. "What's that?" I asked. "The last thing I said was, 'I hate you,' before he walked out the door." I gasped, finally knowing why it was so hard for him to cope with. Imagine that being the last thing you say to someone you love. You never knew what was going to happen. You thought he was coming back and you guys would forget about the fight. But, then he never comes back and you're left with those dreaded words hanging above you, taunting you, for the rest of your life.

"But you were only like," I stopped, doing the math in my head. "Like ten, Evan. You didn't know any better." "So?" he scoffed, still playing with my fingers. "That's an awful thing to say to someone. Not to the mention the last thing you can say to them. If I would have known...Why do you think I say I'm an asshole, Bail?" he asked. "But you were so young. That's the point, you didn't know. No one at that age thinks their Dad's going to go to work and never come back. You didn't even know what was going on that day," I urged, trying to make him grasp that he wasn't a bad guy.

"No. That's an asshole move, Bailey," he stated, not budging one bit. "But Evan," I started, but he cut me off. "Drop it, Bailey," he warned. "No I won't drop-," but he cut me off again. "Bailey,

I said drop it!" he yelled, his fingers seizing from the play time with mine. I knew he was serious so I stopped before I was in too deep. I moved away from him a bit, already noticing how he ripped his hand from mine. I gave myself some space. It was like our unspoken rule before things were confessed. You stopped prodding when you knew it was going to end badly. You didn't prod if you didn't you want to be prodded.

And at this point, I don't think I wanted to be prodded anymore either. This night was emotional enough for the both of us as it was. "I'm sorry," he sighed. "It's fine," I whispered, not looking over at him. I was silently hoping that we could get over this petty fighting once and for all. Having to tip toe around the others' feelings all of the time was getting old fast and I didn't know how much longer I could take not being let in. It felt as though Evan was hiding things from me. It made me feel like I wasn't good enough to be let in, to know those deep dark personal secrets about him that not many knew.

If we couldn't get over all of this hiding, I didn't know what I was going to do. I nestled against my hands behind my back, watching the stars on my own, like he wasn't lying there next to me. I knew he was doing the same, but deep in thought. The thing was, I felt like I knew what he was so deep in thought about without having to ask. We both desperately wanted the person we missed to come back to us, even if had each other. There was one thing I wasn't sure he was thinking about though. I was scared of something I was afraid to say out loud. It was something I was afraid we couldn't get over. It was a thought that had crossed my mind before we had even kissed.

Would I be enough for him, and would he be enough for me?

A couple of hours had past and it was well past midnight when I checked my phone last. Evan hadn't made a move to touch me or even look at me since he yelled at me last when I pushed him. I didn't make any moves either, because I was tired of always being the one making the effort around here.

"I think I'm going to head home," I muttered, picking myself up off of the grass. I was still in my work uniform, a black skirt and light blue colored polo top. I dusted the imaginary dirt off of my bum and waited for him to say something. "Bailey, don't leave," he sighed, sitting up from the grass. He pulled his knees up and rested his elbows against them. He was very attractive looking in his light grey t-shirt and dark jeans but I didn't let it distract me from being slightly mad at him. It was like neither of us could catch a break in this...well whatever this exactly was. "No, I think it's best. It's late anyway," I said, shaking my head. "Your parents are on vacation, it's not like they're worried about where you are," he looked up at me, making my breath hitch at the sight of his green eyes. "I know. But your mom's probably worried and all. It's fine." "Bails," he called to me as I made my way to my car. He was following behind me, mirroring my steps. I finally turned around when he placed his large hand on my car door, forcing me to look at him. "What?" I huffed, jingling my keys in my hand impatiently. I needed time to process if this is what I wanted. I've wanted it for so long, but seeing as how the kiss, us becoming so much closer, didn't even affect his trust in me...well I had a lot to think about. "I can't just leave things...well like this," he gestured a hand between the both of us. His eyes shown in the streetlight with a sadness I hadn't detected before. I wasn't sure if it was because I was walking away from him, or because we brought up his father. "You made things like this," I sighed. I went to make a move for my car but he pressed his hand more firmly into the door, preventing me from opening it. "Evan, let go!" I cried out. "Not until we fix this!" he yelled back, in close proximity. "You're the one who needs to fix this, not me," I said, pointing a finger into his chest roughly. "I'm not the one with a problem." "Bailey, I don't have a-" he started, but was cut off by the ringing of his phone. He pulled it out of his back pocket and widened his eyes at the screen. "It's uh...Leslie," he coughed. He looked up at me like he did the night we almost kissed, like he was expecting me to protest. "I think I should get this. You know, talk to her about everything..." he went on, eyeing me carefully. If it was possible, smoke would have made its way out of my ears from the amount of anger radiating through me then. I clenched my fists roughly at me sides. She was so much more important then finally fixing things with me.

"You know what, Evan? Go ahead. Go talk to Leslie, talk to her about your problems. Because honestly, I'm done waiting around for you to actually say something for once," I said in a low tone, pushing roughly at his arm to get into my car. He looked dumbfounded as I made my way out onto the street, not saying a word as I drove away. The last thing I saw was him put his phone to his ear and his mouth start moving rapidly. I was tired of keeping these feelings of anger, sadness, and resentment so pent up inside of me.

I needed someone to talk to who would actually listen to me. Someone who wouldn't push me out like I didn't matter. I needed someone else to talk other then Evan, because I was so angry with him right now I couldn't see straight. I did the only thing I could think of in that moment. I parked my car over to the side of the road, noting how quiet and motionless the roads seemed at this time of night. I pulled my phone out of my pocket and scrolled through the contacts, stopping at the one name I was wary of. I didn't have a choice anymore. I didn't know if they'd hang up on me when I called, or if they'd even answer at all. But it was worth a shot. "Hello?" I said into the receiver after the second ring. "Bailey? My god," she whispered down the line. "I didn't think I'd ever hear from you again." I felt a stray tear drip down my cheek at the pure remembrance of her voice, and at the memories that suddenly came rushing back all at once. My mind was a blur.

"I know," I sobbed. "I just needed someone..." "You remember my address?" she said, cutting me off. "Yes?" I answered, puzzled. I wiped a few tears from underneath my lids and off of my cheeks. "Why?" "Come over and we can talk," she simply stated. And for the first time in two years, I was making my way to Annabelle Wesley's house to finally make amends with my forgotten best friend.

Chapter 14

I slowed my steps as I made my way up the all too familiar stairs leading up to the big red door. This was the place that I almost called my second home. This was somewhere I could run whenever I ever needed to escape. That big red door held so many memories behind it that I suddenly found myself wondering why I ever decided to leave it behind. I firmly planted my feet against the top step and knocked lightly four times before stepping back a bit.

I felt butterflies graze the ends of my stomach as I waited for her to answer the door. I was nervous beyond belief because I hadn't seen Annabelle in almost three years. I'd practically shut the girl out of my life for good when Lanie died, that I thought she would never want to see me again. Standing on the familiar concrete, cobblestone steps brought me back to the last time I had knocked on that door, just two years ago. It was about a week before Lanie had passed away and I was in need of some box that she told me Annabelle was holding for her. Lanie wanted to check out the contents and such before she died, because she wanted to remember all of the happiest memories from her life.

When Annabelle answered the door, she was all smiles when she saw me, but in her eyes I could see the sadness held beneath them.

She was hurting almost as much as I was because of what was happening to her best friends. She was losing Lanie, and she had to watch me go through so much pain myself. As I was feeling pain for losing my oldest and only sister, she was feeling twice the agony, because she felt the pain her best friends felt. She led me upstairs to her bedroom where she stood on her tip toes and retrieved a pink rectangular box from the top shelf of her closet. As she blew some of the dust off of the top of the lid, I eyed it suspiciously. I had never seen this box in my life, and I was wondering why no one had told me about it before. It was light pink and small, with stickers plastered over all of the edges.

A Polaroid of Lanie and Annabelle was pasted on one side, another of Maisey, Anna, Lanie and Lily on the other. Then, at the top of the lid, was a picture of Lanie and me from her eighteenth birthday party. We were all smiles and goofily grinning at the camera. Lanie's hair was wildly disheveled and mine was matching, with a few strands in my face. That was the first night Lanie met her husband, and the first night I had ever hooked up with a boy. You could say it was a win, win for the both of us. I ran my fingers lightly over the image when Anna handed me the box and let my mind wonder to that night. It wasn't odd seeing Lanie so happy, even when she was lying in a hospital bed a few miles away. She was still smiling and fighting strong, even when she knew the inevitable was upon us sooner than we had ever expected.

That was one of those days where I was wishing to have the brighter traits my sister acquired, and learn to be happy no matter what. Annabelle placed her hand over mine and eyed me carefully. "Now, you know you can't open this on your way back to the hospital," she grinned slyly. I rolled my eyes in return and gave a small smile. That week was the worst for me and I hadn't smiled much at all. It was hard when you knew what was going to happen to your sister and there was nothing you could do about it. "I know, I know, she told me. She said I couldn't open it no matter what and if I did, she would send you to rip my head off." "Good," she smiled. "Tell her there is a letter also from me and a few things from Lily and Maisey as well," she said, lifting the lid open only a bit while she placed the said contents inside.

It was three envelopes, each addressed to their best friend. "Okay," I whispered, feeling my heart swell at the love I knew my sister obtained from everyone. "And tell her..." Anna sniffed, rubbing a hand under the nose. Her eyes were glossy and I knew the waterworks were coming soon. "Tell her that I love her and that I'm thankful for everything that she's done for me." I merely nodded, not knowing what to say to that other than 'okay.' I didn't want start crying myself, because I knew I wouldn't be able to stop. I needed to get back to my sister as soon as possible, because I didn't know how much time she had left. And, with no offense to Annabelle, I wanted to spend as much time as I could with her and not here, crying over the things I've been working so hard to hide.

I left Annabelle's with a hug and tearful goodbye and made my back to the hospital to drop off the mysterious box. I wanted so badly to be in on the secret and know what was inside, but I didn't want to lose the trust Lanie had in me. If I would never know, that was pretty much okay with me, as long as it made my sister happy. And that was the last time I had seen Annabelle. Because of this, I wasn't too sure what I was in for when that door opened. My eyes widened when she opened the door and I was met with those all too familiar blue eyes. Her bleach blonde hair was tied up in a neat ponytail and she was wearing a pink cami with some polka dot pajama shorts. Hers widened as well when she took me in. It's been so long either of us could barely recognize each other.

"Bails," she said, eyeing me carefully. She was shuffling her feet, something she always did when she was nervous, as she waited for me to say something. "Annabelle," I breathed, letting go of a breath I didn't know I was holding. I guess I was sort of relieved that she didn't pounce on me when she opened that door. "It's been way too long," she sighed, opening the door further as she gestured for me to come inside. I nodded along silently in agreement before stepping through the familiar doorway. Her house was much different then from what I remember. They had replaced there plush carpets with hard wooden, light colored flooring.

The blue striped wallpaper covering the corridors were replaced by a cream colored paint that was missing of the crayon stains and scuffs from her younger brothers. I lightly ran my fingertips along the wall as I followed her into the kitchen. She sat in a wooden chair in front of the old dining set and eyed me as I sat down. "So, three years," she continued, playing with her chipped peach colored nail polish. I nodded, not sure what to say first. I didn't know if I should apologize quickly or just pretend that this was normal and talk about my day. I went for the former. "I'm so sorry, Annie. After Lanie..." I mumbled off, not knowing where I wanted to go afterwards. It was hard to say the things out loud that had been replaying in my mind for years. I've had no one to talk to but myself for so long.

"I know," she sighed, looking up at me. She looked like she was on the verge of tears as she took in my face. "I miss her too, you know," she choked. She wiped rapidly under the millions of lashes.

"I know you do," I choked. My own tears were running down my cheeks as we let go of the sadness the both of us had been waiting to share. "I just didn't know how I was going to handle anyone..." I went on, using my jacket sleeve to wipe my eyes. "You could have come to me!" she sobbed quietly, trying not to wake her parents up. "I know better than anyone how it feels! She was one of my best friends, and so were you!" she pointed a finger at me, before ducking her head. "I'm sorry," I breathed.

"It's all my fault. She was just such a huge part of my life that I didn't think..." I sniffed and coughed before continuing. "I didn't think I wanted to see anything that would remind me of her anymore. I didn't want the pity looks!" "Pity looks?" she sniffed, looking back up at me again. "You know I wouldn't do that! I wanted to be there for my best friend. Do you know how it felt when I would call and you would shut me out? How it felt when your mom would shut the door in my face, saying you didn't want to see anyone? I tried so hard, Bails!" I nodded my head, knowing how much I had hurt my best friend. "I didn't mean to hurt you. I didn't want to hurt Lily or Maisey either," I sobbed.

"I just needed some time. But I hate being alone anymore," I went on. "You're not alone," she sighed, wiping the final round of tears from her cheeks. "You always had me and the girls. You have your parents..." she continued. I shook my head vigorously. "I never had them. When Lanie died...they stopped talking to me. It was like they didn't want...didn't want to...even look at me anymore." She got up from the table and wrapped me a tight hug as I cried on her shoulder. I hadn't felt this comforted in ages, and I was regretting all the time I spent away from my friends and the people who I knew loved me. I scolded myself for waiting this long to make things right again. After a while, the crying stopped and Annabelle returned to her seat across the table from mine. She waited until I was ready to finally speak and put her palm under her chin.

”Now that that's out in the open, what made you finally call me?” she questioned. I took in a deep breath; preparing myself to let all of the words I'd been waiting to say, flow out steadily. “I was tired of keeping so much inside. I was afraid to talk to anyone. I felt like no one knew how it really felt. Then I...then I found someone. I found someone to talk to about all of this. It seemed like he got it...” I trailed off. ”He?” she questioned, raising a thin eyebrow. I saw a small smirk appear on her face and shook my head. ”It's almost what you think, but not really. At least I thought it was like what you think. I don't know,” I paused, closing my eyes. So many thoughts and feelings were swimming around my mind and I didn't quite know where to begin.

”What happened?” she asked. It amazed me how she was caring so much about what I was thinking and feeling after how badly I had treated her these past few years. I was expecting this night to go in a completely different direction, one that ended in bruises and yelling. I didn't expect a sit down and her caring so much about me again. ”I don't like talking about how I feel to anyone other than Lanie,” I sighed. “She was the only who seemed to get it. I was afraid to open up to anyone else. I was afraid that...that if I did they would be...taken away from me again.” I averted her gaze, and played with the end of my jacket sleeves while I waited for her to say something. It wasn't everything that I was feeling, but it surely was a start. ”Bails, not everyone you become close with is going to die,” she breathed.

She reached across the table and placed her hand on mine. "Lanie had cancer, something not one of us saw coming. You couldn't have prevented that. But just because you open up to someone doesn't mean they're going to leave you." I looked up at her and she smiled lightly. I smiled back, liking that I could finally open up to someone again. I needed to start letting go again, for my own good. "Now tell me about this boy," she grinned, taking her hand back and jumping impatiently in her chair. I smiled at her and decided to let her know everything.

"Well, his name's Evan," I went on. I continued to tell her everything. I told her how we met at my father's concert and how we got locked up on the rooftop together. I clued her in on how gorgeous he was, just for fun, and then told her how much of a pull I felt towards to him. I even told her about Leslie. "Well why isn't that working out right now?" she questioned. "He won't open up to me at all. I thought that maybe after we kissed," she cut me off with a squeal only a best friend could muster up and I almost jumped. I'd forgotten how she used to do that. "Sorry, I didn't mean to scare you. It's just...nice to see you've gotten back out there again," she grinned.

"Go on." "Well I thought that maybe after we did all of that...that he was opening up more. I thought I could finally get him to trust me. But he doesn't. We brought up his father earlier and he completely freaked out on me." "Bails, you have to realize that you were the same way though. I'm the first person you've completely opened up to since Lanie. He could be scared," she said, shrugging. "I know that. I just...don't know if I could do this if he can't trust me, you know?" I wanted so badly for something to happen between Evan and me, but I wasn't sure if I wanted a relationship with a guy who couldn't trust me at all. The basis of relationships was trust, and without trust...what were you really left with? "I understand, but maybe he just needs time, no? You needed time," she gestured towards me.

"But how much time do I give? He wants to keep kissing me and acting all cute, but he won't trust me. He won't tell me anything," I continued, forgetting to tell her that he was technically still with Leslie. "He had to trust that Leslie girl you just told me about. I wonder why he's not trusting you with things..." she trailed off. "He's also still with Leslie," I mumbled. Her blue eyes widened and she gaped at me. "Bailey seriously?!" "I know! I don't know what's wrong with him," I said, shaking my head.

"He's blind if he can't see what's right in front of him," she said, throwing her hands in the air. "Well he sort of does, but he needs to get his act together. I think you need to talk to him. I mean seriously sit down and talk to him. Tell him everything you're telling me. Tell him how you want him to trust you, and maybe even let him in a little more than you have. That'll show him how you trust him. It may push him to want to be able to make whatever you guys have...work." I nodded my head in agreement, already running a plan of what I would say to him through my head. It would be hard, telling Evan things I've only talked to Annabelle about. But if I really wanted to make this work with Evan, I would need to do this. And I would need to do this right. "Thank you so much for talking to me and listening, Annabelle, seriously," I quickly said. She smiled small at me and shook her head. "It's not a problem. I'm just glad to finally have my best friend back."

"Again, I'm so sorry for doing that to you. You didn't deserve that. I promise not to do that anymore. Now that...now that I know I

can talk to someone other than Lanie...things will be different,"
I smiled. She got up from the table and I followed suit, as we
wrapped each other in a hug. It was like a piece of my heart was
being built back in, knowing I had my best friend back again. It
felt like things could possibly become easier now that I had some
sense of normality back in my life. I was going to make a change
for the better this time. "Now go talk to that man of yours, and
let me know how it goes!" she squealed, pushing me towards the
front door.

"I will," I grinned, wrapping her in another hug. "Thanks again,
Annie." Before I made my way back to my car, we agreed to slowly
form our friendship back together again and made plans for a
shopping date with Lily and Maisey later on. When things finally
became settled in the other aspects of my life, she said to give her
a call so we could set it up. She said she wanted things to finally
come back in full circle again for me, so I could deal with one thing
at a time and actually be completely happy again.

I pulled out of her driveway and made a right, making my way
back to my house for the night. As I drove down the silent roads,
I pulled out my phone and dialed Evan's number. It went straight
to voicemail so I assumed he was still on the phone with Leslie.
I forced the small amount of anger inside of me downwards as I
took in a deep breath. "Evan, it's Bailey. When you get this, come to
my house. We need to talk...and I mean really talk," I said, before
ending the call.

I didn't know how this conversation was going to go, but I knew
it needed to be done. I needed to finally fix all of the drama in my
life and make things right. I wasn't sure if Evan and I would ever
see each other again after this conversation. I didn't even know if

he would want to see me after I said all that I had to say. He needed to know that I couldn't continue anything if he wasn't going to trust me, and I needed to let him know that I would try if he would too. I was in for a long night.

Chapter 15

"Evan, it's Bailey. When you get this, come to my house. We need to talk…and I mean really talk," I replayed the message she left me for the eighth time that night. I stared at my iPhone's screen like it had the answer to all of my problems and everything I was thinking. Bailey and I had left things on a pretty broken note, and I wasn't sure what to expect when I hopped into my car and drove down the familiar road leading to her house. A part of me was expecting her to just push me completely out of her life once and for all. The other part of me was expecting a mind blowing kiss, followed by a massive amount of apologies. I was really hoping for the latter.

To have someone in your life like Bailey Keys was something everyone should wish they had. I may have acted like a Class A asshole, but it wasn't intentionally at all. I was just so used to being on guard with my feelings when it came to those around me. When it came to Bailey, it was like my guard was dropped completely, and it made me say things I regretted. She only itched for more about my past, and that was just something that I couldn't give her. And I really wanted to give her what she wanted.

As I stopped at a red light, I turned the volume up on my radio a little bit so I could hear the song that was whispering through the speakers. It was Yellowcard's song, "Only One," and my eyes widened at the hit home lyrics that poured through the car. It was as if every situation surrounding my red head beauty was described and I didn't even need to decipher it to the bone. It was amazing the kind of affect music had on people, their situations...their lives. I tapped aimlessly along to the song on the steering wheel and accelerated down the road. My mind was running in rapid circles, trying to picture what was about to go down at the Keys' house in about five minutes. I know I had some serious apologies to divvy out, but then again, I didn't know if I could do it.

If I apologized, it would only make her think that I had changed my mind about opening up about the past...which I definitely had not. I couldn't give her what she so badly wanted, and I didn't know how that would affect her anymore. There really was only so much someone could take before they broke. I pulled up to the house and parked in the massive driveway. All of the house lights were off, except for one that I recognized came from Bailey's bedroom on the east wing of the home. I glanced up at her window, hoping I could catch a glimpse of her. When that failed, I took out my phone and texted that I was outside in the car, waiting for her. It took a few moments before I saw her bedroom light go off and her come through the red oak doorway in front of the house.

She walked over to my car and I shut off the engine, sticking the keys in the back pocket of my jeans. She crossed her arms over her chest tightly and shivered slightly at the cold of the night. It was almost three in the morning and she was suited for bed just like any average person at this ungodly hour of night. Her plain white tee hugged her curves nicely and she matched it with a pair of pink polka dotted pajama shorts. It was a late summer night, but the wind made it almost feel like you could catch a cold if you sat out here for too long. I so badly wanted to hug her when I got out of the car, but I knew she wouldn't let me without apologizing first. So I figured I would begin with that, and work my way up from there. "Bails, I'm so sorry," I sighed, shaking my head. I shoved my hands into the pockets of my jeans and looked right into her eyes.

It was the first time I actually looked at her face and I was shocked to see that she looked like she'd been crying earlier. Her eyes were masked in red and they were puffy. "Have you been crying?" I went to make a move to touch her face but she stepped back before I could even reach her. She shook her head and wiped underneath the rims. "No," she snapped. "I'm fine. What are you apologizing for, being a jerk or hiding so many things from me?" I widened my eyes at her attitude and immediately put up a wall I wasn't expecting to put up earlier. This night was already starting off far from what I was thinking in the car ride over here. "Are you kidding me? We talked about this before." I sighed, rolling my eyes.

She scowled at my childish expression and stepped only a few inches towards me, leaving a substantial amount of room between us. "Yeah, we did. But that didn't solve anything," she seethed. "So we're going to talk about it again, Evan." I leaned against my car causally, waiting for her to start another idiotic fight with me again. "Let me have it," I said, motioning her onward with a hand. "Stop acting like such an arrogant jackass. You know you're in the wrong here, but I no longer am." "What's that supposed to mean?" I questioned, raising an eyebrow. She was just as much at fault as I was. That was when she broke down completely. "I opened up to you, Evan!" she shrieked. Her voice seemed to carry to higher decibels seeing as it was so much quieter at this time of night. If she didn't tone it down, she would be waking up her parents and the neighbors in a few minutes. "Sh!" I scolded, coming up to her and placing a firm hand over her mouth.

I covered her protests as she tried to push me off of her. "Get the fuck off of me!" she shouted, finally succeeding in pushing me off. I fell against my car with a small thud, and turned to look at her with surprise written all over my face. "What the hell is your problem, Bailey?" "My problem?" she breathed. "My problem seems to constantly be you, Evan Warren!" "Bailey, you really need to..." She cut me off with her rant again. "No! It's my turn to talk now. You had your chance!" I was about to cut in and tell her that I hadn't had a chance to explain anything since she'd yelled over me, but I thought ill of it and kept my mouth shut. "I trusted you with my secrets! I told you about all the pain I suffered from Lanie and her stories!" she cried, her face turning a light shade of pink as the tears started to fall and her body started shaking.

"I thought that maybe...just maybe a guy like you would finally get it, you know? I'd be able to have someone to find comfort in, someone who would tell me that it would be alright, and actually mean it! You've been nothing but a closed-off asshole that has dragged me along for months! I don't know how I could have been so stupid!" "Hey, I didn't drag you along!" I shouted back in protest, finally deciding to say my peace. I should be able to have a shot at saying how I felt about all of this shit too. But Bailey wasn't letting me have it. "Yes you did!" she cried, wiping away a stray tear that had fallen past her cheek and down her neck. "You're even still with Leslie after all of this!" "You know I can't just..." "Shut up and let me finish!" she screamed, getting a little bit closer to me. I backed against the car, not sure what she was going to do.

"You don't push someone to open up to you, and then not do shit in return, Evan," she seethed. "I trusted you with my deepest of thoughts and you can't so much as talk about Aaron without acting like you've spilled some government secret. Newsflash, jackass! Everyone has a past! You can't hold onto everything like it would kill you to let go. Because guess what? It does end up killing you either way. It eats away at you, slowly and painfully. It gnaws at your heart and your mind until you want to rip them out to save yourself from it all. It eats away until you've finally realized that you've had enough and it's time you do something about it. Keeping that pain in, Evan, is what kills you.

Not letting it out!" I stared at her wide-eyed at first, not too sure how to respond to words like that. It definitely had hit home for me, and I actually had a gut wrenching pain hit me straight to the core. It killed me to see her freaking out and breaking down like this. But she needed to understand that it wasn't as easy for me as it was for her. "Bailey," I urged, grabbing onto her shoulders. "Unless you plan on finally opening up to me, get your hands off of me," she warned slowly and softly. Her tone held a slight evilness to it, which I determined could only come from a place that hurt her deep down. I was the one causing her all of this pain. I was the one doing this to her. I slowly released my hold on her and gauged her reaction. When she finally realized that I wasn't opening my mouth and my hands had left her body, she merely nodded. It was an official sign that she had given up on me, just like so many before her had done.

"I...can't..." I mumbled, my voice strained and laced with hurt. I wanted so badly to open up to her and give her the relief she needed. I was the one making her feel so bad and I had the capability to stop it. But I couldn't will myself to do it. "I can't believe you," she whispered tightly. She put her hands up in surrender and turned to walk away from me. She stopped in her tracks for a second and turned to face me again. "It's been years. When will you finally learn to just let go?" she questioned, her eyes trained on mine. They were begging me to say something...anything to make this moment better than what it had started out as. When she said those words to me, though, I felt the wall drop slightly and anger from somewhere deep within me bubble up to the surface. "You don't get to say that shit!" I seethed angrily, my hands clenching into fists at my sides. If she had been a guy, she would have been on the ground, clutching at her face.

But this was Bailey, and I couldn't hit a girl no matter what they had said or done. But I could punch something else. I slammed my fist into the driver's door of my car. "Damnit, Bailey!" I shouted. "Fuck you for even saying that to me!" I continued. I held onto her eyes with a growing vengeance and watched as her pained and surrendered expression turned into that of a frightened and shocked girl. "Evan..." I cut her off. "No! Now it's my turn to speak. You don't get to say shit like that to me, when you know exactly what it feels like to lose someone close to you! Do you know what it's like to have your father die without even getting the chance to say goodbye?" I yelled on. I didn't care if it was three in the morning.

I didn't care if neighbors around us were sleeping and probably calling the police to report a domestic assault. I cared about settling the score and making her pay for what she had said to me. No one gets to disrespect me and tell me to let it go. Who can let go of their dead father? "I don't care if it's been twelve years or twelve days! Losing your father doesn't just disappear! Do you know how many times I replay that moment inside of my head? Do you know how many times I've wished I could do it all over again? So I could say sorry, or so I could even say goodbye before he walked out of that door?" I carried on. My chest was heaving from the anger and the yelling, and my fists were still clenched, ready to hit another car door again.

"You don't get it! So don't try to justify anything to me! A sister is a whole hell of a lot different from a father, Bailey! You can't stand there and honestly ask me when I'll let it go. That's pure and utter bullshit. I'll never ever let that go. And for you to ask me to do that, well that just makes you a complete bitch," I seethed the last word like it was venom dripping from my tongue. Her eyes were wide and she looked so riled up. It was like an attack dog was being released from its leash and it was ready to pounce.

"You've had years to get over it, Evan!" she screamed, coming at me and pointing a finger into my hard chest. I ripped it away and threw it aside, staring her dead in the eye. "And you got to say goodbye," I whispered angrily. "That's what so different from me and you, Bailey. You knew." "And that makes it any better?" she yelled, as fresh tears masked her face and rushed down her neck. She didn't bother to wipe them away this time and threw her arms up in the air.

"She died right in front of me, Evan!" "You knew," I stated, simply shrugging my shoulders. "She withered away right in front of my eyes!" she cried. "You don't know what it's like to have someone you love, die right in front of your eyes for days on end, knowing you can't save them. You were too young to understand what was going on!" Before I could even think, words spewed from my mouth so quickly that it reminded me of the morning in 2001. I was desperately wishing I could have a do over.

"Lanie wasn't half the person my father was. It's different," I scoffed. My own eyes widened in disbelief at what I had just said to her and I felt my stomach drop to my feet. If I could replay that moment, I would take it all back and say something that tried to solve this mess. I would try to make her understand. I wouldn't be this cocky, arrogant son of a bitch that just said something like that to someone so hurt. "Oh my god, Bailey I didn't mean to..." I rushed, but she cut me off with a simple raise of the hand. Her face was flushed from its original tainted pink and a third batch of fresh tears framed her lids. I was such an asshole. "I'm done, Evan," she simply stated, putting emphasis on done.

Her voice was scratchy from the screaming match and oddly calm. But if anyone was sitting in my exact spot right now, they'd see that her eyes read those of hurt and heartbreak. I couldn't believe what I was doing to her. You would think that after all these years; I would finally learn to think before I opened my mouth. I should have known that words can't be taken back, especially words of that vicious kind. I didn't understand why my mouth sometimes ran faster than the rational part of my brain. I completely destroyed something that had made me so utterly happy for the first time in years. I was getting so good at being the bad guy. It was becoming like a second nature to me to be the king of fucking things up.

"Bailey," I called, reaching a hand out to her now retreating figure. My head was spinning with the things I should have said, instead of those crappy ones. I ruined it all. And now I couldn't take it back. I watched her as she slowly padded up her porch steps and softly shut the door behind her. Her eyes were filled with tears and slowly spreading over her face. I felt a piece of myself break along with her, and I had never experienced something this close to bad before. Not since hearing about my dad's death from my grandmom that night in early September. Nothing had come close to this pain since then. The pain was something I felt for her, but for myself as well. I was reprimanding myself so hard that I was left with no confidence.

I didn't understand why I decided to do the things that I did. I hated that I managed to be such a terrible person to those who I cared about the most. I stared at her door for a few more fleeting moments before opening my car door and slowly putting it into reverse. I backed out slowly from her driveway, knowing it would most likely be the last time I would see Bailey or this house ever again.

I needed some type of guidance, some type of comfort. I didn't want to wake up Aaron at this time of night, even though I knew he wouldn't care. He would gladly open the door for me when I arrived and invite me in for a late night beer. But this was different. This feeling I had was something so far from what Aaron and I had talked about lately that it didn't seem right to be at his house. I needed somewhere else to go to chase away these nasty gnawing feelings. As a last minute decision, I made a right turn on the next intersection and made my way to the one person who I knew I could talk to about this feeling. This feeling that was too familiar for my own liking. I went to visit Lieutenant Warren.

Chapter 16

"Sweetie, what's the matter? I heard shouting," my mother urged, letting herself into my bedroom, unannounced. "I'm fine. Everything's fine. Can you just leave now?" I sniffed. My face was pushed against my pillow as I clutched it tightly in my hands. My hair was matted to my face and skinny red strands kept getting trapped in between my lashes. I'm also pretty positive that my face was as red as a tomato. I felt the bed sink next to me and still didn't make a move to look at her. I wished she would go back to being the inattentive mother she was just yesterday. I really wasn't up to talking to anyone right now.

"Bailey, what happened?" she sighed. I felt her hesitantly touch my back, before she placed her hand fully onto my back. It was like she was questioning whether or not it was the right, motherly thing to do. "I said I don't want," I snapped, but she cut me off. "I do not care," she simply stated. "Your noise woke me up at three in the morning and I'm going to find out what it was." I moved my face from the pillow and looked up at her through tear stained lashes.

"You wouldn't understand," I said, keeping firm eye contact with her. She couldn't just pick and choose when to become a parent. Life didn't work that way. "I'm trying to," she pushed, tentatively moving a piece of hair from my eyesight. I eyed her carefully, trying to decipher what was actually going on here. She was never this doting before and I wasn't sure how to handle it all right now. "You're choosing now to try and make things better?" I questioned, raising a thin eyebrow. I sat up in bed a little, readying myself for this conversation.

"Well...yes. I wasn't sure how to...well how to approach this topic Bailey. It's not that easy," she said slowly. "It wouldn't have been this hard if you didn't make it this way," I deadpanned. She sighed heavily and ran a hand through her long blonde locks. It was the only time of day anyone would see her without her hair tied up in a too tight bun on the top of her head. She let the locks fall for bedtime and that was all. "I know. You're father and I talked about a lot of things that have been worrying him.

You were the first thing he spoke to me about." I stared blankly at her, confused. My dad was definitely not the type of man to stick up for himself when it came to my mother. He always felt it best to steer clear of the arguments and just give her what she wanted. The fact that he was the one who approached her completely shocked me. "Dad talked to you...about me?" I questioned while my brain tried to wrap itself around the idea of my dad actually sticking up for himself. What was with everyone surprising the hell out of me tonight? "Yes he did. And I wanted to apologize for how I've been neglecting you since..." she trailed off, looking behind me.

Her eyes met my bedside table where the picture of Lanie and I was sat. I was twelve and Lanie was sixteen in the picture, and she was sporting a pink and silver tiara for her birthday party. My mother's eyes brimmed with tears as she looked on. "Since she died," I sighed, letting out a breath I didn't know I'd been holding. She merely nodded at me and wiped quickly at her cheeks before continuing. "I didn't mean for things to become this...terrible, Bailey. I'm sorry for being so cruel to you," she cried. The waterworks were in full force now and I found myself tearing up just watching it unfold before me. "It's okay, mom," I said, lying my hand on top of hers. She gripped it with her other hand as she cried. "It's not," she choked. "I should have fixed this sooner. Everything around us was just crumbling and I was too wrapped up in..." "Can you at least say her name for once?" I urged, feeling traitor tears start to caress my cheeks.

"I miss her, you know?" she continued, completely bypassing my question. I only let her off the hook because I was curious as to what else she was going to open up to me about. It was so much emotion to deal with for one night that I didn't know if I could handle anymore bearing of hearts. "I do too," I choked. She squeezed my hand briefly before moving on. "I promise you," she said, eyeing me carefully to make sure she had my full attention. "I promise you that I will fix this, sweetie. I will do it." I could only nod at the sincerity in her voice and smile briefly. She opened up her arms for a hug and I gladly complied. It was the first time we had showed any such emotion to each other since before Lanie's news of the cancer spreading and I was relishing in the familiar feeling. I had missed this side of my mother so much that I didn't want to let go. I was afraid this would be the last time again, and she would return back to being the completely self-centered mother she had been for the past two years.

I wiped a hand underneath my nose as we pulled away and I saw her smile small. I didn't think she full understood how happy I was that she was willing to fix our relationship. It was like my life was sort of coming full circle, just like Annabelle was hoping it would for me. Everything seemed to be working out. Everything except...Evan. Evan. I had forgotten about our little fight for a mere moment while my mom and I were patching things up. I had forgotten about the sadness that was washing over me before my mom had walked through my door. I felt my stomach plummet to my feet just like it had when Evan scoffed those few little words. Those few little words that were full of so much disrespect and anger.

When he compared Lanie to his dad, saying that she was never the person his father was, it was like a shot to the heart and knife in the back all at once. My mind went blank and my eyes stayed trained on him for a few moments, trying to gather if I had heard that right.

How could someone be so cruel?

I didn't care if he rethought his words or accidentally let them slip. You shouldn't be allowed to hurt someone that way. It was as though I was seeing a brand new Evan, one I hadn't seen since day one. I wasn't used to seeing him so riled up and mean before, and it definitely wasn't my favorite side to him. Just reliving all of the gory details in my mind was making me tear up again and I had forgotten that my mom was still sitting on my bed beside me. "Bailey?" she questioned, placing a gentle hand on my shoulder. "What's the matter?"

It was the second time she asked that question and the second time where I wasn't so sure that I wanted to answer it. She had no idea what she was in for when she asked such a question. I didn't know if I should tell her about Evan or my feelings about Lanie from the past two years. We were just starting to patch things up and I wasn't sure I was ready to let her in like that just yet.

I shook my head and murmured a small, "Nothing," before lying back down again.

"I thought we were going to work on the whole mother-daughter issue, Bails," she urged, looking down at me worriedly.

"We are. I just...don't think you'd understand right now," I sighed. She didn't seem mad like I thought she was going to be, but she still held a worried look to her. The amount of things she didn't know of could have gone on forever, which I definitely didn't have the time or patience for. I hadn't let my mother in for almost three years and I wasn't sure I was ready to. I was just starting to open up to Annabelle and Evan.

Two people seemed like enough for right now.

"Alright," she huffed as she got up from my bed. She leaned down to kiss my head. "Just remember, I'm willing to try to make this work. I want to fix what happened to us. Just say the word and I'll be there in a flash," she smiled. I nodded my head in response before turning my face back to my pillow. I was waiting for my bedroom door to click shut, but it never did. I waited some more to see why she was hovering.

"Lanie loved you so much," she breathed. I heard her voice closer than expected and rolled over to face her. She was next to my bedside again and was clutching the picture from my table. She stared longingly at it for a long time.

I was completely shocked that she had finally said her name out loud. I hadn't heard her say it since the last day Lanie was in the hospital. It was as though that after she died, my mom didn't want a reminder anymore. So she stuck to keeping herself busy with clients and court work, and made sure Lanie's name stayed out of her mouth.

"To infinity and beyond," I grinned, looking down at my wrist briefly before meeting her eyes again. She smiled down at the picture and rubbed her finger over Lanie's face.

"You two were always coming up with weird sayings like that," she said.

"We were the perfect partners in crime," I noted, my mind winding back to the memories from when we were little. Everything came back in a whirlwind.

"Oh my goodness," my mom gasped. She held a hand over her mouth and closed her eyes tightly. "I can't believe I forgot about it." "What?" I asked quickly. What had she forgotten that Lanie suddenly reminded her of?

"The box," she simply stated, like that was supposed to mean something to me.

I stared at her blankly for a few moments, trying to figure out what a box had to do with Lanie. After a minute or two, my mind suddenly flew to the day when I visited Annabelle and gave her the pink box. I had just been thinking about it the other day and I didn't know why I hadn't questioned it before. After I gave it to Lanie last, she never spoke of it again, nor did anyone else for that matter. It was like the box disappeared, never to be found again.

"What about the box, Mom?" I urged, practically on the edge of my seat. Was I finally allowed to see what was inside of it? Was I finally able to be let in to all of the secrets? "She told me to give it you," she went on, opening her eyes widely to look over at me. I couldn't believe she forgot to give me something so precious and worth while. It was obviously one of Lanie's last wishes, and she completely forgot to let me know.

"She did?"

"Yes," she pointed a finger at me, "She said for you to read the letter inside carefully when you were ready. She wanted you to have it after she was..." she trailed off. I didn't urge her to continue because I knew where she was getting at. Before the waterworks began again, I pounced off the bed and anxiously bounced up and down on the balls of my feet. "Mom, where's the box?"

"My room, in the closet on the top shelf. I'll go get it," she quickly said before jetting out of my room.

By now it was almost four in the morning. I was full of energy and anxiousness that I couldn't contain myself. I had dropped the events with Evan from my mind and completely focused my attention on Lanie and what she had left behind for me. There were things for me inside of that box and I was excited to see what she had written for me.

A couple of minutes later my mom came rushing into my room with the familiar light pink box in hand. It was decorated in shiny, child like stickers like it was the last time I saw it. The only difference was that the box wasn't as sharp and new like it had been the day I took it to Annabelle's house. It was a little worn on the edges and some of the stickers were slowly wearing away.

She handed it to me gently and smiled again. "I'll leave you to it then. I'd better be off to bed." I only nodded, not even looking up at her. My eyes were trained on the box and my mind was wondering what she had left for me, what she had to tell me, what she left for only me to see. It was a box full of surprises and secrets compiled into one.

I was holding Lanie's life in my hands.

I sat slowly on my bed as my mother shut my door behind her. I sat cross-legged with the box in my lap for so long, I had lost track of time. For being so excited, I didn't know where to start or if I should even open it. Now that it was in my hands and I was allowed to view what was inside, I was frozen with fear. I was fearful of what I would find.

Would there be things that made me think differently of Lanie? Were there words inside that would hurt me or make me upset?

It wasquarter after fivewhen I finally decided to open the box. I played with my phone for a while, horsed around my laptop and put away folded clothes for almost an hour. I was trying to figure out when and if I should open it up, and was clearly wasting all of the time I could.

I gently lifted the lid with both hands and placed it onto the side. The small box was full of folded up pictures, Lanie's toy story key chain from her key ring, her wedding ring, pictures of her and Brayden, her favorite baby blue cashmere sweater, her birthday tiara, a diamond bracelet my dad had gotten her, the bottle cap to her first beer, a mix cd of her favorite songs to drive along to, my favorite box of gummi worms and an envelope with my name grazed across the front. I fingered the items inside gently, one by one. I opened up pictures from Lanie's birthday parties and family gatherings. I even remembered one we took the night before we snuck out of the house for the first time to go see amidnightmovie premiere.

I smiled at the memories before picking up the last item I hadn't opened yet. I ran my fingers across her familiar curly handwriting before flipping the envelope over. On the flap were the words, 'Eat the gummi worms while you read this,' with a huge smile next to it. I opened up the not so fresh bag and stuck a red and green one in my mouth. I gently ran a nail underneath the flap to open it up and slowly took out the papers inside. As I ate the candy, I read the letter carefully.

Dear Bails,

I wonder how long it took Mom to give you this box? Knowing her, it was probably almost a year since everything happened. But just know, this box was meant for you to see in the long run. I know Maisey, Annie, Lily and I made it look like this huge secret. I took out most of the pictures of all of us and our special things and replaced them with ones of me and you and my life basically. You know this box was pretty much the key to my life, and I realized you were the hugest part of it.

My eyes welled up at the last part and I grabbed a tissue off of the side of the bed before continuing.

We were the perfect partners in crime, huh? I'll miss those days with you the most I think. Being locked up in this hospital wasn't what I expected my life to turn out to be, but life hands you crap you can't change sometimes, doesn't it? I always tell you to smile, no matter the situation. You were always the more emotional one of the two of us!

Take it from me, the girl who's hoisted in some room with four white walls and a television to stare at all day. Life can turn out to be something you totally never expected, so grab what you can and make it your bitch! (: No, but seriously, you can't go around being unhappy all of the time. You have the world's most beautiful smile and you need to show it off more often than you do! You're an amazing person, Bails, and you should never doubt that for a second.

What I aimed to do in this letter is hand you some lessons that I've learned in my short lifetime. My first one is about trust. Because we all know you're not one to open up to anyone...ever! Learn to see the world as good and bad. There'll be some people you can trust, and others you can't. They'll be honest and caring, or cruel and deceiving. But that's what your judgment's all about. You need to open before you can figure out who to trust. Without me there, well you'll be alone if you don't choose to talk to someone. I'm watching you, and you know I'm pissed if I see that.

Another lesson that I feel is most important, is love. Open yourself up to love someone else Bails. Love doesn't just come and go. It comes at the most unexpected and beautiful moment, that you can't just let it pass you by. You know I'm a firm believer in fate, and I believe fate coincides with love. I can probably bet all of my most cherished items that you're reading this whole speech about love when you needed the guidance the most, aren't you? Fate's doing its job then (; If there's some gorgeous boy out there whose got you heart right now, don't let him go. Even if he is a complete screw up. Give him a chance, and see where it can take you. I did the same with Brayden. He wasn't always such a saint! Don't over-think for once in your life and go with what your heart tells you. You don't have time to waste, Bails, believe me.

Always remember that I'm here for you whenever you need me, even when I'm not physically there. Just talk to me when you need to vent, let it all out of your system and I'll be there to listen. I love you baby sister, and never ever think otherwise. Go out there and live your life to the fullest and happiest extent you can. You can do it.

To infinity and beyond,

Lanie

I clutched the several pieces of paper in my hands firmly as tears streamed down my cheeks and neck. I didn't bother to wipe them away, seeing as they wouldn't stop to begin with. I reread the letter over and over again until I could practically recite it by heart. She was right, as Lanie was always notorious for being. I needed to give people a chance, and stop taking things to extremes.

My first step in doing so was making amends with Annabelle. My best friend was there for me through thick and thin and I shut her out because I thought I knew what I was doing. I thought it was what was good for me at the time. I was slowly starting to learn that I wasn't really good at making rash decisions. I still needed some type of guidance from Lanie, even when she wasn't here.

This letter was like a final wrap up of every piece of advice she could ever give me to steer me into the right direction. If she was no longer here to help, I could always go back to this. It was the main two components I always seemed to struggle with in my life. I realized now that I needed to be happier whenever I could, and move on from the struggles I was facing. I needed to stop dragging myself down with sadness just because she was gone.

I needed to do it all for her.

The only step I seemed to have trouble with though was one that involved a certain selfish boy who had hurt me the most. I wasn't sure what to do with him, considering he chose to spew me bullshit after bullshit line to make me upset with him. I needed to figure out what I was going to do about the boy I had fallen for and finally get my life back in order once again.

Evan was the final piece to the entire puzzle to settle.

Chapter 17

"**D**ad, this is shit. I can't deal with it all anymore," I whispered into the air. I was sat in the grass amongst the familiar tombstones lined up in crooked rows around me. The night was deep black and hid the names of beloved lost ones and their quotes on the cold stone. I picked at stray blades of grass with nimble fingers while I absentmindedly continued a conversation with my silent father. The one way conversations always seemed to soothe me at my darkest hours.

"She was the only one who understood what I was going through. Now she thinks I'm some jerk who doesn't care about her. I mean, I know I'm a jerk, especially after what happened with...me and you..." I trailed off, roughly throwing a blade of grass into the pile before me.

It was times like these that I really missed my dad. I could deal with the baseball games as a kid where he wasn't in the stands, the missed bedtime stories at night, not being able to eat his famous pasta with meat sauce, not hearing his laugh, or even his blinding charm with others around him. I could deal with him not being here for those moments. But I most certainly couldn't deal with not having my dad here to guide me. My mom was always telling me how much she loved me and was always there to talk if I really needed it, but it wasn't the same growing up. A guy couldn't exactly ask his mom what was going on with puberty or how to ask a girl out without getting coddled.

A boy needs his dad for moments like those. And moments like these were the most important.

"I don't know what to do about it," I sighed agitatedly. "I want her to trust me. God, I want to trust her," I breathed.

I felt lower than low when I left Bailey's house earlier tonight. She needed someone to give her comfort, someone who knew exactly what she was going through. I was the one who was supposed to be all of those things for her and I failed her. I failed her just like I had failed everyone else in my life.

My dad was the most perfect example.

"Do you think I should try to talk to her?" I asked, staring his tombstone in its center. "She probably wouldn't even answer my calls," I mumbled, shaking my head. I ran a frustrated hand through my hair and let out a breath. I really needed to figure this out.

"I really wish you were here right now. You'd probably tell me to man up and blame it all on myself so she'll take me back or something," I smiled small. "Do you think she'll even try to forgive me?"

I stared off behind his stone for so long that I'd lost track of time. So many scenarios of how I could apologize and what I would say to make it better ran through my mind. Every time seemed to end the same, with her still hating me and me wallowing in my own self-pity. She needed to understand why I couldn't fess up about the things of my past. She needed to know that I needed her as much as I knew she needed me.

Off in the distance was the faint sound of crickets chirping softly. The wind around me was picking up and I kept having to throw my hair out of my face to keep it away from my eyes. I found myself wishing I could talk to Bailey as easily as I could talk to my dad. She would understand things so much easier if I could. She would get why I thought so low of myself, and she would see that I actually do care so much about her. I never cared about someone else so much in my life and it quite frankly scared the shit out me just to think about it.

It was safe to say that I was falling in love with that little redheaded spit fire.

"Dad, what do I do? Give me a sign of something that'll help me out here," I begged, racking my brain for more things to do or say to make this all right again.

Here I was, a twenty one year old man, crying to my dead father about a girl I loved who clearly didn't love me back. To any passerby, I'd look like a pathetic piece of shit.

My phone chose this time to beep quietly, mixing with the faint sounds from the hidden creatures in the bushes. I pulled it out slowly, knowing it was probably just my mother, wondering where the hell I was atfive o'clockin the morning. She wouldn't rest until I was home, even if I was considered a legal adult.

As I unlocked the screen, Bailey's name popped up and my eyes widened. My heart pounded in a way I'd never felt before, and I felt myself being scared but incredibly happy that she was at least making the effort to say something to me.

'I'm willing to give you another chance to explain yourself. If you're willing to fess up, meet me at my house tomorrow morning around 10.'

I reread the text message more times than I should have and wondered what made her change her mind. When I last said those stupid things back at her house, she honestly seemed like she was done with me for good. I thought I'd never be able to see or talk to her again and it was officially over. The fact that I was actually getting another chance made me the happiest I'd ever been. And I couldn't help but wonder if this had something to do with a sign from my dad.

I looked up from my phone and trained my eyes on the stone in front of me. "Thanks Dad. I couldn't do any of this without you," I smiled.

I got up from the dirty ground and brushed off the back of my jeans briefly. Before I made my way back to my car, I tapped his stone a few times with my fingers in praise.

"You watch out for me so much, Dad. Watch out for little Greg too, please. He needs you far more than I do."

At that, I made my way back to my car and headed for home for the night. I knew I wouldn't be able to sleep because I knew I was seeing Bailey in less than five hours. My brain was already trying to figure out what would happen. But, as my mind wandered back to that text, my heart sped up a little bit.

This would mean that I finally had to own up to everything. I would have to let her know what happened with my dad, and why I felt like such a jackass all of the time. I would finally have to let her in. People just don't get second chances everyday. I had to do this if it meant that I was getting her back, I had to.

This was going to the hardest day of my life.

The whole night I lied awake in my room, not being able sleep a wink just like I had expected. I cleaned a few things up and ate a ton from the kitchen until it was time for me to shower and get ready to see Bailey. I left my house atquarter to ten, starting the car and heading for the Keys' mansion.

The entire ride over, I was sweating through my white collared shirt and wiping my palms consistently against my jeans. My heart was beating a mile a minute in my chest, warning me that this wasn't my time to say anything. Meanwhile, my mind was telling me that this was the time to fess up to everything. If my heart wanted Bailey, it would need to shut the fuck up and let me talk when I stepped up those stairs.

I pulled up the paved driveway, taking a deep breath before shutting off the engine and getting out of the car. I tapped my fingers nervously against my leg as I walked up the pathway to the cheery wooden door. I knocked three times as slowly as I could. While I waited for her to answer, I kept playing with my hair and making sure my clothes were in place so I looked presentable.

I was shocked when an unfamiliar woman opened up the door and gave me a shocked look back.

"Who are you?" she questioned, raising a blonde eyebrow. She was dressed in a purple silk robe, her arms across her chest.

I swallowed loudly. "Um, I'm Evan. Who are you?" Shit that sounded really rude. She didn't even know who I was.

"I'm Mrs. Keys. This is my home. Why are you here at…" she checked her watch briefly. "Ten in the morning?"

"Bailey…she uh…told me to come over," I stuttered, wringing my hands nervously.

"Oh," was all she said, her eyes trained on me, taking me in. Her eyes widened for a moment before she said, "Please do not tell me you are the thing that made her cry last night."

I widened my eyes at her remark and looked everywhere but her. Shit, did Bailey tell her about our fight last night? Was she going to kick me out of her home before I even got to see her?

"Uh, I might...have been," I mumbled, choosing not to lie to anyone anymore. This was my time for a change. I might as well start with her mom.

"Of all things pure and holy," she sighed. "Why would she want to see you after you made her fall apart the way that she did?"

I gulped and racked my brain for something to get her on my good side. I didn't want to risk being kicked out before I could tell Bailey everything I had to tell her. I knew last night was going to haunt my ass.

"I uh..." I started, but was cut off with that all too familiar voice from behind Mrs. Keys.

"Mom, I didn't fall apart," she sighed. I grinned when I saw her come out from behind her mom and she looked at me. "You're early."

I nodded in agreement. "I know. Just didn't want to be late."

She rolled her eyes and pushed her mom lightly away from the door. "Mom, I have this under control. You can go finish making breakfast for Dad."

She eyed me suspiciously for a moment before walking towards the kitchen. I looked back at Bailey expectantly, hoping to see some kind of sign that she didn't hate me.

"Let's go up to my room," she said, gesturing for me to follow her upstairs. She was dressed in a pair of denim shorts and a pale yellow shirt that hung off of her shoulders. She was notorious for wearing shirts like that, and it made her look all the more beautiful to me.

She closed the door behind us before she sat down on the edge of her bed, giving me the same expectant look that I had just given her downstairs. This time though, I knew she was expecting me to talk. I took a deep breath and wrung my hands for the thousandth time that morning before starting.

"I'm so sorry about last night," I started, eyeing her carefully. "I didn't mean to say any of that shit."

She glared at me. "You already said sorry. You're here to tell me other things I don't already know."

"I know," I sighed. "But I need to know...do you forgive me?"

"I can't give you an answer to that question until you start telling me what you supposedly can't," she said, crossing her arms over her chest defensively.

I closed my eyes briefly while I took another much needed deep breath. You're doing this because you love her, asshole, I kept telling myself. I opened my eyes and looked straight into her gorgeous hazel ones. God I really hope she forgives me after all of this.

"My dad died in 911," I started.

"You already told," she went to cut in, but I raised a hand to stop her.

"I know. I'm just...starting from the beginning. Give me a chance."

She widened her eyes at my firm hold on the conversation and nodded slowly. I took it as my queue to continue.

"Before all of that," I sighed. "We had gotten into a...fight. I told him I hated him because he took my favorite truck. I didn't clean my room like my mom told me to, so that was my punishment. This is why I feel like such an asshole when I talk about myself. I never saw him again after that. That was the last...the last...thing

I said...before he died," I said in a rush, closing my eyes to take it all in.

My mind flashed back to that morning and I felt my heart squeeze viciously. I never want to think about that.

"Evan..." she breathed. "You were only ten. You can't..."

I cut her off again. "The only reason I want to actually re-live that day is because I want another do over. I want to say 'I love you, Dad' instead of 'I hate you.' But I...can't," I said, my voice strained.

"You can't blame yourself," she continued. I opened my eyes to see her giving me a look of pure concern. My arms ached to reach out and wrap my arms around her, but I wasn't sure if she'd allow me to do that just yet. I most likely wasn't forgiven.

"I can though!" I yelled, throwing my hands in the air angrily. "You don't get it, Bails. Your dad's still here. Mines not! I can't take it all back! The last thing I said was 'I hate you!' That's a pretty fucked up way to say goodbye!"

"But you didn't know!" she fought back. She got up off of the bed and walked in front of me. My head was ducked in shame and she lowered herself to look into my eyes. "You didn't know," she breathed.

"But if I would have," I breathed.

"You didn't know," she repeated. "There are no buts in this situation."

"Just...this whole situation...my life...pisses me off," I scoffed. My eyes were still trained to the floor, but Bailey remained standing in front for me.

"Why does it piss you off?" she questioned quietly.

"Because I can't change what I've done! Day after day, I'm an idiot with the decisions I chose to make! I let every person I've ever known down. Hell, the only reason Aaron's still here is because he knew what I was going through and he had sympathy for me!"

"Then why not let anyone in," she urged, grabbing onto my arms tightly.

I finally looked up at her before I spoke up again. "Because it scares the shit out of me! I hate talking about how I feel. I'm not some poetry snob who can easily spew shit out, making it sound like a damn song. It's not easy for me to say this stuff to you, don't you get that? I'm doing this because I love you and I'm fucking scared you're going to leave just like the rest of them. But at this rate I wouldn't blame you for the rotten shit I've done!"

After the rant was finished I took a deep breath and raked a hand through my hair roughly. It froze in mid air when I realized all of what I just said and I was immediately frightened. My heart pounded uncomfortably in my chest as I figured out what to say to make her not freak out. I looked up into her bright hazel eyes, noting how wide they were as she stared back at me.

"You..." she started. "Love...me?" she asked, pointing a finger from myself to her.

I swallowed roughly and merely nodded my head. I knew I was going to regret telling her all of this. I knew I was going to ruin it by saying something I knew she probably wasn't ready to hear. She didn't even feel the same way as I did, and I already ruined it all.

"You," she started again, her voice at a normal level this time. "Love me?"

"Yes," I mumbled, scared as to what else she was going to say. She repeated it like she couldn't believe I was saying this to her. Hell, I probably scared her from this relationship...or whatever it was, for good. I was so good at messing things up for myself that I deserved an award.

"Wow," she breathed. "I wasn't expecting that."

"Me neither," I laughed nervously, sticking my hands in my pockets. I was dreading what else she was going to say. She was definitely going to kick my ass to the curb after all of this, I knew it.

She stayed silent for what felt like ages and I was literally writhing in anxiety. If she was going to deny any feelings for me, I'd rather her do it now and save me the time of freaking out.

"Say something," I urged, my voice covered in nerves.

"I just wasn't...expecting you say that. I mean, I was expecting you tell me to eff off and never ask you to fess up about your past. God, even that was surprising that you actually opened up to me," she breathed, tucking a red strand of hair behind her ear.

"Surprised me too," I noted, watching her with careful eyes.

"I can't believe you blame yourself for all of that, Evan. You need to know that you were a kid and you can't blame yourself for saying something like that. You didn't know he was going to leave. You know full well that if you knew, that would not be the last thing you would have said."

I nodded. "I know. I just...wish it could have been different. I'm sorry for taking so much out on you this whole time. I didn't mean it in the slightest. All of those things I said..." I trailed off.

"You didn't mean it when you said 'I love you,'" she quipped, raising an eyebrow at me.

"No! I meant that! I mean, yes I love you. I just didn't mean to say it right now," I mumbled the last part. I couldn't meet her eyes after that. I still didn't know how she felt about this whole thing.

"Then why did you say it?" she asked, hands firmly placed on her hips. She was determined to make this so hard for me.

"I don't know!" I yelled, throwing my hands in the air again. "I was frustrated and it just...came out."

She nodded her head slowly. "I'm happy you told me," she said.

I raised my head quickly as she smiled lightly at me. "Happy I told you that I love you, or happy that I told you about my dad?"

"Both really," she grinned, coming closer and placing her arms around me tightly.

I quickly followed her actions and wrapped my arms around her lower back. I rubbed my thumbs gently against the small amount of skin showing underneath her shirt. I felt a warmth spread through me that I wasn't used to in the slightest bit. But I knew it was something I was ready to get used to.

"Does this mean that you..." I started, knowing she knew where I was getting it. She still hadn't told me how she felt and I was still writhing with anxiousness at what she was thinking.

"I love you too, Evan," she whispered against my shirt. I smiled widely at her confession and pulled her away from my chest.

Before she knew what I was doing, I leaned down and placed my lips against hers. She smiled into the kiss as she kissed me back, running a hand through my hair. She pulled against the end, just like the last time we shared a kiss and I growled in approval into her mouth. I was in this state of happiness that I'd never experienced before.

"Thanks for not leaving my ass when I did so much to you," I said as I pulled away from her lips, unwillingly. I didn't want to stop, but I really was happy that she didn't leave like everyone else in my life, and she needed to know how much I loved her for it.

"I was going to at first," she said, making me frown.

"You were?" I asked, my arms still wrapped her waist.

She nodded. "Yeah, but someone told me it was better to give people second chances. You already had like three, but I figured I'd try one last time," she smiled, playing with the ends of my hair affectionately.

"Well I need to thank this person for changing your mind," I grinned back, fingering the end of her shirt with my fingers. I lightly grazed her skin and noticed her skin covered in tiny goosebumps.

"You can thank her," she breathed, looking over a picture placed on her bedside table. I squinted at the picture, noticing it was two girls. One was a familiar redhead and another was a blonde girl, who looked to be a little bit older than the former.

"Who's that?" I questioned, trying to figure out who she was.

"Lanie," she whispered, staring longingly at the picture.

"How did she…" I went to ask, but she shook her head and kissed me briefly.

"That's something for another day. Right now, I'd rather you just kiss me," she smiled, pulling me back down to her.

"Yes mam," I grinned, meeting her lips with mine quickly.

We continued making out for most of the morning, not letting things get too far with us just yet. I relished in her closeness to my body and never wanted to let her go. She would never understand just how grateful I was that she decided to stay. I could finally have someone who understood what the death of a loved one was like. I finally opened up to someone other than my best friend and my mother and it was an amazing feeling. All I could think as I kissed her was how much I actually loved her and how much I owed my dad for his guidance through this.

I realized I could do this without him here. I could be happy for once and not blame myself for the stupid shit I'd done in the past. If I could open up to Bailey, I could finally open up to those who I pissed off in the past. I could live life without regretting every move I made.

I could do this. I could conquer this.

Chapter 18

I was in a state of pure euphoria for days after Evan's confession. We'd spent the remainder of the morning making out on my bed before we fell asleep next to each other for the major portion of the afternoon. Both of us had confessed that we hadn't slept a wink the night before, so it was expected that we'd be tired eventually. I woke up later in the day with his arm planted firmly around my waist like he was afraid I was going to leave him before he woke up.

At this point, I wasn't planning on leaving him for a long, long time.

"Five more minutes," he groaned in my ear when I tried to get up.

I smiled at his protest and kissed his cheek before removing his arm. He growled in response and pulled me back down. I giggled like a school girl as I tried to move out of his grip.

"No," he simply stated, smiling with his eyes still closed.

I rolled my eyes at his boyish traits as I let my head hit the pillow once again. I let my eyes run over his face as he slept, noticing all of the things I hadn't before. It was my first time properly getting a look at his face other than when we kissed, and I was surprised to see a light dusting of freckles across his nose and under his lids.

I ran my eyes down to his full lips and went to lean in for a kiss before his words stopped me.

"Done checking me out yet, creep?" he smiled, opening his eyes to take me in.

I pushed his shoulder roughly and couldn't help but smile back. "I was not."

It was his turn to roll his eyes now. "Oh okay."

"You know," I said, completely ignoring his teasing. "You're sleeping in my bed and my mom still doesn't know who you are."

He widened his eyes at the mention of my mom and looked almost frightened at the thought.

"She scares me," he admitted, playing with the hem of my shirt.

"She does not," I scoffed.

"She does too. She looked like she wanted to throw me in the oven instead of your dad's breakfast."

I giggled at his idiocy and flicked him in the nose. "She just doesn't know who you are."

"Did you really cry like that over me though?" he asked, concern wavering in his features.

I lowered my eyes, not confident enough to look him in the eye. "Not really."

He brought a hand to my cheek gently, trying to pry my eyes back to his level. "I promise to never hurt you like that again. I'm trying here, Bails. But I never want to see that look again on your face."

"What look?" I questioned.

"That look of pure disgust with me," he mumbled, looking away from me now.

I placed a hand on his that was on my cheek. "I know you're sorry."

"You sure? I mean I was an ass to you, I deserve to," he continued, but I cut him off.

"Stop it!" I scolded. "You said sorry and you're forgiven. With a confession like that earlier, how can I not forgive you? You've been through so much; it's easy to see now why you blame yourself so quickly all the time. I'm not going to give up and leave like everyone else, Ev."

He grinned widely at my statement and pulled me to him for a quick but passionate kiss. I'd never experienced such a kiss before. Who knew that a kiss so small could speak so loudly? After he kissed me, he pulled me to his chest closely, running a hand gently up and down my spine.

"I'm proud of you for opening up to me, Bails," he said.

I pulled away from him to look him in the eye. "Shouldn't I be saying that to you?"

He shrugged his shoulders. "Maybe. But I am proud of you. I know how hard it is, believe me. And you haven't had the time I've had to grieve."

I nodded shortly before cuddling back into his chest as he played with my hair. I could stay this way forever, but I knew I needed to get up and show my mom I wasn't get up to any freaky business while she was home.

"We need to go see my mom," I stated, pulling away from him again.

He squeezed my waist tightly. "But I don't want to," he whined.

"She's going to think we're getting all...you know...in here. We've been up here for hours."

"Well I don't know if I can last hours. Maybe close to an hour..." he trailed off, grinning playfully as he skimmed his fingers against the skin that wasn't hidden beneath my shirt.

"Shut up," I said, shoving him off of me.

"What? Weren't you the least bit curious?" he questioned, still keeping that playful grin on his lips.

"Alright, let's go see my mom," I said, louder than normal. I pushed him off of me and straightened out my clothes.

"You look fine. You don't look like I roughed you up at all," he said, rolling up the sleeves of his button down.

"My god, Evan!" I yelled, throwing open the door and pushing past him.

"I'm joking!" he called back to me as I made my way down the stairs.

I walked into the kitchen area, stopping in my tracks when my mom and dad were seated at the dining room table. My mom sipped lightly from a cup of coffee while my dad was eating a sandwich furiously.

"Geez Dad, you act like mom hasn't fed you in days," I quipped, walking slowly over to the refrigerator door.

I pulled it open, taking out two water bottles from the top rack. When I shut the door, Evan was standing behind me, the smile completely gone from his face. I smiled at his frightened features and turned to my parents.

"Guys, this is Evan. Evan these are my parents, Phil and Liz," I said, gesturing between the three of them.

My dad eyed Evan with a hardened gaze, taking him in fully. I could practically see Evan swallow hard at the look my dad was giving him and couldn't help but laugh. I covered my mouth to stop myself.

"Son, sit down," he said, putting down his sandwich and offering him the chair in front of him.

Evan eyed me warily before taking the seat and looking back at my dad. Phil eyed him seriously for a few moments before picking the sandwich back up again and clearing his throat.

"Now Evan," he started, taking a large bite. "What are your intentions with my daughter?"

"Well sir," Evan started.

"Call me Phil. You make me feel old calling me Sir."

"Phil," he coughed. "I want your daughter to be my...girlfriend."

"Really now?" he questioned, placing the sandwich back down. My mom smiled affectionately beside him.

"Yes," he stated. I could see from my place by the fridge that Evan was wringing his hands absentmindedly on his lap underneath the table.

"You plan to treat her right?" he asked, crossing his arms on the table in front of him.

I smiled affectionately at the whole scene before me. For years, my parents had always treated me like I hadn't matter when Lanie was in the picture. Even after she died, they still pretended like I wasn't there. I spent years trying to gain an ounce of attention from them, to see something that showed me that they cared enough for me. This moment showed exactly how much my dad actually did care for me. I wished for moments like these, where my father would pressure a boy I was about to date. He would make sure he was good to me, and scare him into being a doting boyfriend.

Then last night, my mother opened up to me for the first time ever. When she finally said Lanie's name, I knew that things were changing and she wasn't pretending anymore. She was ready to make amends and figure this mother daughter relationship out. I was ready to get my life back in order and make everything normal for once in my life.

I'd say this was off to a pretty good start.

Later on that evening, after my dad was finished interrogating the hell out of Evan, we headed for our place. My dad quizzed him on the do's and don'ts of being my boyfriend and asked him over and over if he planned to treat me right. At the end he said, 'I won't take any bullshit. Don't cross me. Got it?' All Evan could do was nod before silently pleading me with his eyes to get him the hell out of our kitchen and somewhere safe.

We spent the remainder of our day in the backyard of the theater, the place we always seemed to return during and after every turning point in our relationship. We'd spent countless hours in this lawn, talking about things over and over. We'd spent minutes arguing over what now seemed like the stupidest things to me. But now that I think about it all, it only brought us closer together in the end.

"I'm happy we're at the point we're at right now," he murmured close to my ear.

I was lying in the grass with his arm wrapped around my waist. My hands were lying limply against his chest as he played my hair gently. I breathed in deeply, taking everything in.

"Me too," I grinned, dancing my hands along his stomach.

"Did you know I have a tattoo too?" he asked.

I stopped dancing my fingers along his stomach and propped myself up to look at him. "You do?"

He nodded before lightly moving me to the ground. He sat up on his elbows and undid the buttons of his white shirt. I watched as he shed the shirt and removed his right arm. My eyes immediately met the large print etched into his skin on the upper shoulder. I squinted in the little light from the streetlights and tried to figure out what it said.

"It says Ladder 24 above the gold badge. Underneath it is my dad's name in red," he whispered, eyeing the tattoo.

I moved from my seat on the ground to lean over his body and get a good look at the tattoo. I ran my fingers over the tattoo gently, just like he had done to mine not that long before. I let then run slowly over his father's name, Gregory Warren, written in neat cursive lettering.

"It's beautiful," I murmured.

"That's why I kept questioning you about yours," he admitted, going to put the shirt back on again. As much as I loved the sight of his shirtless front, it was pretty cool tonight so I couldn't blame him.

"Why didn't you tell me sooner?" I asked, returning to his opened arm. I fell into place against his side.

"We got into a fight before I could," he said.

"Ah, yes the fights," I noted.

His phone started ringing from his front pants pocket and he used his free hand to pull it out. Our eyes matched as they widened at the name on the screen. I had completely forgotten about her.

"Leslie," he read, not making a move to answer the call.

I immediately became angry as I pushed away from his body. "You haven't dumped her yet?"

"Fuck," he muttered underneath his breath. "No."

"No?" I breathed, aggravated. "You're kidding me right?"

"I'm sorry, Bailey," he pleaded as the phone quit ringing. Not a moment later it beeped, signaling a voicemail she had left.

"So you're cheating on her with me again?" I questioned, pushing further and further away from him.

"No! Well yeah, sort of. But I completely forgot about her because I all caught up in the stuff between me and you!" he urged, making a move to come near me.

"Don't touch me!" I barked, pushing his hands away from me.

"Bailey, please! I didn't mean for this crap to happen. I'd meant to break up with her, but then you called and we got into that fight. I spent the whole night at my dad's, trying to figure everything out. Then we talked and I did all that stupid ranting. Look, I'm sorry!"

"Save your sorry bullshit for someone who cares," I said getting up from the ground and brushing my butt off.

I went to walk away from him but he beat me to it and pulled me to turn around. I stopped in my tracks and threw his arm off of me.

"Please Bails. You have to believe that I didn't mean for this to happen. I don't even like her!" he pleaded, his eyes prying me to forgive him.

"Then why haven't you broken up with her yet!" I yelled, throwing my hands in the air in frustration.

"I forgot about her when I was with you, honestly!"

"This always happens," I scoffed, crossing my arms in front of my chest.

"What does?"

"We're incredibly happy for a few hours before you go and screw it up again!"

"But I don't mean to at all, Bailey!" he urged, making a move to touch me again. "Please, let's just talk this through. I promise I can fix it."

I moved away from him again and put my hands up in surrender. It was like déjà vu how eerily similar this was becoming compared to last night.

"When you get your priorities straight, Evan, then come and talk to me. Right now, I don't have time for this bullshit," I said, before walking off and leaving him by the side of the wall.

As I walked towards the pavement, I realized I had no car and no way home. Evan had driven us with his car and I figured he would just drive me back home. Now I had no idea what I was going to do. I took out my phone and scrolled through the contacts, trying to figure out who to call as I walked down the dark streets.

The minimal streetlights down the paved sidewalk made it seem much more eerie and haunted looking then the usually pleasant neighborhood in the daytime. It made me much more cautious as I turned my head at every slight cracking noise or flutter of a shadow behind me. The more I became scared, the quicker I scrolled through the names. I wasn't in the mood to hear my parents asking so many questions and I wasn't really talking to the other friends who were present in the list.

So I settled on the only name I was up to talking to.

"I'm on some creepy street around the corner from the theater downtown. Can you pick me up?" I sniffed, noticing stray tears making their way down my cheeks. I didn't want to let myself cry over him again.

"Why are you there?" she questioned. I heard light rustling noises and the drop of keys as she moved around on the other end of the phone.

"Evan and I got into a fight and I left him," I said, wiping away at more traitor tears. I couldn't believe this was happening all again. "Now I have no way home."

"Didn't you just text me saying you guys patched things up?" Annabelle asked as I heard a door shut behind her.

"Well he decided not to break up with that slut Leslie, so no. Things are not fine."

"That son of a bitch!" she snapped. "I'm on my way."

After she hung up, I found myself on the contacts page once again. When I went to click out of it, Lanie's name was dead center in my eyesight and I felt more tears fall for her. It was moments like these where I needed her the most and wished she would come and rescue me from the pain. I called her house phone, knowing Brayden never disconnected it. It rang for a few moments before landing onto the voicemail and I let out a sigh at her voice.

I used to do this all the time after she died, relish in the comfort of her voice through the phone. It was the only way I could hear her voice anymore. Brayden didn't disconnect the voicemail she left at their house because he liked to call it once in a while, like myself, to hear her voice again. It was still on, even after these past three years. It was amazing how much everyone in her life felt for her.

I replayed the voicemail over and over as I waited on the corner of some oddly named street. It was long and I could barely read it with the minimal light I was given. Her voice through the phone gave me the comfort I needed. I wasn't scared that I was sitting in the dark with no one around. I wasn't wallowing over Evan for the few brief moments she talked to me.

"Hi, this is Lanie. I'm probably out enjoying something other than my house," she would say, followed by a giggle. "God, why are you calling my house phone anyway? I'm never home," she scoffed playfully. "Well, just leave a message after that beep and I'll get back to you eventually!"

I let it beep another time, ending the call and calling her again. I kept doing it until Annabelle showed up, pretending my sister was next to me giggling the way that she did over the phone.

It was times like these that I really needed my older sister.

Chapter 19

I stared off into the distance for what felt like hours. My feet were firmly plated where she had left me moments before, frozen to the concrete. I could have chased after her; I could have tried to explain further. But it all felt useless anymore. She wouldn't believe a word I said to her either way, and I quite frankly couldn't blame her.

My phone buzzed in my pocket, followed by my obnoxious pre-made ringtone. I rolled my eyes, knowing who it was without having to check the caller ID.

"What in the hell do you want?" I sighed heavily as I answered.

"Well that's no way to talk to your girlfriend," she scoffed.

I ran a hand through my hair, frustrated beyond belief. If I was going to do it, I needed to do it now. I couldn't hold back anymore. I couldn't drag this one-sided relationship any further than this point.

"I'm not your boyfriend," I muttered slowly, gauging her reaction. The momentary pause over the phone felt so prolonged, I was wondering if she had hung up on me.

"Yes you are, silly," she giggled, but it sounded forced and fake.

"Not anymore, Leslie," I simply stated. I could do this. I had to.

"What the hell are you on about, Evan Warren?" she sneered.

"I'm done. I can't do this anymore. I don't want you to be my girlfriend."

"But why!" she shouted. I held the phone away from my ear for a moment, wincing at the harsh tone.

"I just can't do it anymore. The feelings aren't there like they used to be," I lied.

I never really felt anything for Leslie other than physical attraction. We didn't connect on any other level other than sexual, and I wasn't about that kind of life anymore. With Bailey around, I found that there was way more to a relationship than just physical attributes. Leslie wasn't the one I wanted to share my time with anymore.

"You're kidding me, right?" she gasped.

"No, I'm not. Leslie, we're done."

"That's not fair! Don't I get a say in this?" she shouted again. I could hear the hurt clear in her voice and it made my chest tighten up just a bit. I wasn't used to being this cruel.

"I'm sorry, Les, you don't," I said, not really knowing what else to say after this.

"This is because of that stupid bitch Bailey, isn't it?" she questioned. The hurt was fully erased from her voice and was now replaced with a kind of fury I wasn't used to hearing from her.

"That's not why I'm," I started, but she cut me off.

"Don't lie to me Evan! This is totally about her! You've been ogling her since day one!"

"That's not true," I scoffed.

"It's so true! Stop being such an asshole and tell me the truth for once in your life," she continued.

"Fine!" I shouted, giving in to the anger bubbling up in my insides. She wanted a fight; I'd give her a fight. "Yeah it's about Bailey! I fucking love her alright? I'm done with you Leslie. You don't give a shit about anyone but yourself!"

"You're an asshole, Evan Warren. I'm done with you!" she shouted before hanging up.

I took the phone away from my ear and looked at it with wide eyes. I didn't expect the conversation to go down that way, especially with her acting like she'd broken up with me.

I wasn't feeling empty, upset, or even remotely different than from what I was feeling five minutes before she called me. I was just...distant. I couldn't grasp onto what I was going to do with everything going on in my life. Leslie was gone, but I knew she would be back to seek some type of revenge against me.

The only thing I could hope was that she didn't go anywhere near Bailey.

A few days later, I'd had enough of moping around and being ignored by Bailey. I threw on a pair of skinny jeans and a clean shirt before hopping into my car and speeding down the roads to the Keys' house.

I'd stayed in my house for days, wondering where the hell to go from here. I tried to call multiple times, but was met with her voicemail over and over. I had texted but wasn't answered. I even tried Facebook, but was left with no hope. She was taking this thing way too far and all I'd wanted to do was fix it.

I pulled up into their driveway, quickly parking and throwing my keys into my back pocket. But, when I got up to the front steps, I took my time, carefully taking the steps one at a time. I raked my brain for the right words to say when she answered the door, making sure it all sounded right. I would stop at nothing to get her back.

I pounded the door with three hits, wringing my hands uncomfortably while I waited for someone to answer it. My heart was running a mile a minute, making me think someone could hear it through my chest. I'd never been this nervous in my life and it was scaring the hell out of me.

I just needed to make things right.

"Well look who it is," the familiar blonde woman said, opening the door further when she noticed who I was.

"Mrs. Keys, I really need to talk to Bailey," I quickly blurted out.

"And as a mother, why do you think I should let you come into my home and talk to my daughter?" she questioned, raising an eyebrow. She placed her hands on her hips and eyed me carefully.

"Because I'm a screw up and I want to make things right with your daughter…" I continued, praying she'd let me in and let me explain myself.

"I don't want you here," I heard my favorite voice say from behind her mom.

"Bailey, please," I breathed.

She came out from behind her mom and mimicked her, placing her hands on her hips. "I want nothing to do with you," she spat.

"Bails," I went on, but she cut me off.

"I've had enough of your explanations for why you keep screwing up. I'm done playing games," she simply stated.

"But I need to tell you that I," I said, but she cut me off again.

"Unless you came here to tell me that you've gotten rid of Leslie and you have proof of that, I don't want to hear it. Especially when I know you'll be lying to me anyway," she said.

"How do you know I'd be lying?" I questioned, suddenly curious.

By now, her mom had left with a death glare in my direction before she scurried off to the living room. Bailey and I were left alone to argue once again. Bailey pulled out her phone from her back pocket and scrolled through it for a moment. When she finished, she tapped the screen twice and flipped it over so I could see the picture plastered on the front. My eyes widened in recognition as to who that was and what they were doing and I immediately went into explanation mode.

"That's not recent at all!" I yelled.

She flipped the phone back over and eyed me for a few moments. It was a picture of Leslie and me making out on her bed, but it from almost two months ago. On the bottom in bold white lettering were the words, "If he was really yours, why would he have slept over at my place a few nights ago?"

"It's not?" she quipped, sarcastically. "Then why would there be a picture of you wearing the same blue shirt you wore the last time we were together while lying on top of her?"

"Bails, I swear to God that's not from a few nights ago. That was from months ago. I broke up with her the night you left me at the theater!"

"I don't believe you," she scoffed.

"You have to!" I shouted, flailing my arms about.

"And why should I?!" she questioned loudly, getting in my face. "You've done nothing but keep secrets from me since day one, Evan!"

"I'm not lying to you Bailey! I've never lied to you! I've kept certain things from you, yes. But I've never lied to you," I breathed. "Please, just let me in so we can talk about all of this."

"I'm afraid I can't do that," she simply stated, making a move to shut the door in my face. I placed a foot in between the door frame and the door itself, stopping her.

"Bails, please," I mumbled, desperately.

"You had sex with her, Evan," she said, keeping the door stuck at a minimally open view.

"But I didn't a few nights ago," I pleaded. "I had sex with her over two months ago. Ever since things have been going on with you, I haven't slept with her once. I broke up with her that night you freaked out at me. I was an asshole and an idiot and I'm sorry."

"I'm sorry, Ev. I can't believe a word you say to me anymore," she said sadly, before kicking my foot out of the way and shutting the door in my face.

I stared at the door for a few more minutes, wondering if I should knock again. I wondered if I should just walk into the house like I owned it, grab her and kiss the life out of her. But the more I stared at the door, the more I realized that no matter what I did, she'd never believe a word I said to her anymore.

There was absolutely no way she would believe me.

I slowly walked down the stairs and slammed the car door shut as I got in. I cranked the stereo to a rock station with lots of drumming and guitar solos before driving away from the house. I beat my fist against the steering wheel angrily, tired of keeping my feelings in anymore.

Leslie was screwing up my entire life. I knew she would seek revenge eventually, but I didn't think she'd do such a shady thing like this. I didn't even know she had taken that picture while we were kissing that night. Even if I had known, I didn't think she'd have enough guts to send such a picture like that. With that picture in Bailey's possession, there was no way I was going to be redeemed for everything I'd done to her.

I drove off to Aaron's house, a plan slowing forming in my mind to get Bailey back. I needed her back, no matter the circumstances and I knew Aaron would be the one to help me.

"I get what you're saying, bro, but I don't think this is the right thing to do," Aaron said, warily.

"I need to do something to get her back, Aar," I muttered, desperately.

"So you think the best way to do that is expose Leslie?" he questioned.

"Well...yes I do," I said, shaking my head.

"That's not the way to do it. Bailey needs time. Not some high school shit to happen and you make Leslie out to be a slut. Things don't work that way. Relationships don't work like that" he scoffed, smiling.

"Then tell me what to do, Aaron!"

"I'm not the one with the answers. You know her way better than I do, Ev. You have to figure it out," he explained, shaking his head. "Maybe try talking to Leslie again?"

"No," I scoffed, waving a hand. "That would never work."

"You never know, man. She could change if you really tell her how you feel about everything."

"She'll throw it back in my face and do something else to piss me off. That's just how she is," I told him, feeling a slight sickening feeling in my stomach at the hopelessness that was dripping from this conversation.

"Wow, that Leslie of yours sure seems like a bitch," he laughed, crossing his arms in front of his chest.

"She's not mine, asshole," I seethed, shooting his a glare.

"Well either way, she was yours. I never did agree with your choices in girls," he laughed, crossing his arms in front of his chest.

"Bailey's not a good choice?" I asked, raising an eyebrow.

"I wouldn't know. You haven't brought her around," he quipped, glaring at me.

"I've meant to, a lot of times actually. We just keep fighting..."

"Maybe you guys just aren't right for each other, man," he said, getting up and slapping me on the back.

"We are dude! You don't get it. She gets things like no one else I know. I need her back," I said, frowning deeply at the memory of everything going on.

"Well good luck, Ev. I don't know how you're going to do it. I'm not helping you with this one though. Because I don't agree with this," Aaron said, shrugging his shoulders.

"I'm going to get her back. Just you watch bro," I said, getting up from the table and grabbing my keys from his kitchen counter.

"Whatever you say," he scoffed, following me outside of his house and to my car. "Just be careful. You might be the one who's going to get hurt here," he warned.

I turned around to face him and glared. "What does that mean?"

"Just watch yourself. You're not the only out there. She could move on without you man," he simply stated, walking back into his house with a wave of his hand.

I got into my car, angrily shutting the door behind me. There was no way she could move on that fast. She told me that she loved me just like I loved her. You don't give up that easily on the people that you love. She couldn't do that to me...to us.

Could she?

Chapter 20

For days after receiving the text message from Leslie, I cried on and off. There were times when my dad would tell me a joke or my mom would keep my mind off of things with shopping, but my mind always ran back to that picture. It was like my body was shocked to a stand still and my mind was on a time freeze, forever stuck on the past. It taunted me, showing me that it was impossible to move on from the returning idiot who broke my heart.

The emotional days went on for a while, I suppose, until I was invited to a party by Annabelle. She told me it was high time I went out and was introduced to new places, new people and try new things. I honestly couldn't blame her for pushing me so hard to get out of the house, seeing as though I haven't left much at all in the past few years. The only times I did were for school, work and seeing Evan. But this time I knew I needed a fresh change in my life and I decided it was time for me to go and meet new people.

It would be a hell of a lot easier to get my mind off the stupid boy running circles around my brain.

"I'm here," Annabelle sang as she let herself into my bedroom door without a knock.

I was lying on my bed, cuddled up underneath my purple duvet, staring off into the wall. My hair was a mess, seeing as I hadn't really found the determination to get up and take a shower. I was wearing the same pajamas I went to bed with a few nights ago, and I hadn't even taken the time to brush my teeth. It was probably a horrid sight for Annabelle to see.

"Jesus, Bails. You look like shit," she noted, placing a bag full of hidden items onto the foot of my bed and taking a seat next to it.

"Thanks," I muttered, not making eye contact with her.

"C'mon," she said, tapping my leg with a hand. "Get your butt in the shower and get ready to go. We're leaving in an hour."

"An hour?" I groaned. "That's not enough time to do anything," I said, throwing the duvet off of me and raking a hand through my greasy strands.

"Oh it is. I can get you ready in half the time if you hurry up!" she yelled, hitting my arm. "Now go!"

I rubbed my arm where she hit it, frowning at her. "Fine, I'm going."

After a relaxing warm shower, I wrapped a towel around my body and scurried towards my bedroom. Annabelle had laid a very revealing outfit out on my bed while I was gone and a few accessories to match. I eyed her warily.

"What is all this?" I asked.

She looked up at me with innocence plastered on her face. "An outfit of mine I'm letting you borrow for tonight. I picked out some accessories from your draw to match it, I hope you don't mind."

"That looks a little...revealing, don't you think, Anne?" I asked carefully, pulling on underwear underneath my towel. I turned my back as I dropped the towel and put on a matching bra, waiting for her response.

"Not at all as revealing as mine might be," she winked at me when I faced her again.

"I'm not trying to get molested tonight," I noted, running my fingers across the fabric of the short skirt on my bed.

"I'll be taking excellent care of you tonight, don't worry. This is just to attract some much needed attention to your beautiful self while we're there. You need it," she explained, patting my back comfortingly. "Now get your butt in these clothes so I can fix your makeup and hair."

I obeyed silently, with a scowl clear on my face. I wasn't really up for partying at some unknown person's home tonight. I'd much rather be swaddled up in my bed sheets and watching old romance films than be grinded up against by some pervert who wanted to 'get it on.'

This was definitely not how I wanted to spend my Friday night.

"Woo!" some guy shouted again, right near my eardrum.

Annabelle had dropped us off at the party almost an hour ago and I was already ready to leave and be back in my bed. I wasn't ready to be with a room full of people, pushed against walls and sweaty bodies just yet. It was my first party since Lanie died, and without her here to rescue me if I needed it, well it was a pretty scary thought. Even though Anna told she'd take good care of me tonight and watch my back if I needed it, she was nowhere to be found.

She'd last left with some muscular boy with too much cologne on, and I hadn't seen her since. She just giggled at his whispering in her ear and called to me that she would be right back to keep a look out for me.

So much for that.

"Hey baby girl, you want to dance?" a deep, husky voice whispered into my ear.

I felt his breath glide against my ear and shivered at the contact, almost horrified. His hands found their way around my waist, pulling me against his hard chest. He tried to move my hips against his, but I wouldn't budge.

"No thanks," I yelled over the music. I tried to remove his hands from my body, but it was doing me no good. It was like they were glued onto my hips, forever locked on.

"Come on. I can show you a very good time," he growled.

I pushed my head away from his lips and made a move to budge out of his grip. When that failed, I came up with a lie. "Well I was just about to get a drink. Could you go get me one?"

"Sure thing. I'll be right back gorgeous. Don't go anywhere," he warned playfully. I merely nodded in response.

When he turned his back to me, I made a run for it to any empty room I could find. The bathroom was occupied, by what sounded like a couple going at it against the door. I ran upstairs towards the bedrooms where the noise seemed to diminish somewhat as I made my way up. The main bedroom's door was locked, so I knew it was no good to force myself in. Then, when I turned my back, there was only one door left on the floor, so I silently crossed my fingers that it was open and safe.

I slowly made my way across the hall to the opposite bedroom and turned the golden knob gently. When it clicked open, I let out a sigh of relief and quickly shut it behind me as I went in. It was pitch black, the only light seeming to come from the moon outside the window. The moonlight slithered onto the bed, not doing my sight any good as to where the light switch was. I blindly ran my hands along the wall near the doorway, but failed at finding what I needed.

Then a lamp on what seemed to be a computer desk flicked on and my heart jumped in my chest. I clutched at my chest, my breathing becoming heavy.

"Guessing you needed to be alone, too?" the deep voice asked.

My eyes flicked to the boy sitting on the computer chair, a beer propped up on the desk in his hand. He had shaggy, brown hair that stopped just beneath his brow and bright blue eyes that seemed to pierce right through me. He was dressed in a dark blue thermal and a pair of jeans that met at the bottom of his Converse clad feet. I took him in slowly, trying to calm my still rapid beating heart.

"You scared me," I breathed.

"Sorry, that wasn't my intention," he smiled sheepishly. "Just figured I'd help you out."

"Well thanks," I muttered. "I guess I'll go now, seeing as though this room is occupied too."

I made a move for the door, my hand resting on the knob, when he stopped me.

"No wait!" he called, softly. "Don't leave. You could stay here with me if you want. I mean, I don't bite."

I turned around slowly, meeting his piercing gaze again. If my heart hadn't been set on Evan, this mysterious boy would have seemed like a very cute replacement.

"I just..." I started, my breathing still heavy. I took a moment to settle down, noticing how the bass thumping through the floor matched my erratic heartbeat. "I just needed to get away from all of that."

I suddenly became well aware of the fact that this was starting to turn into the night where I met Evan, except we were on a rooftop, not a bedroom. I didn't know what was with me, how I kept meeting mysterious, strange boys in odd places when I needed to escape. It was like a hero at the end of the tunnel. Except, I wasn't sure I wanted this strange boy to be my hero too; especially seeing as how the first boy worked out.

"Me too," he grinned, fixating his gaze on the bottle of alcohol in his hand. "It can get pretty crazy down there."

"I wouldn't know honestly. I haven't been to one of these in ages," I confessed, settling down onto the bed before me.

"And why is that?" he questioned, raising an eyebrow at me.

"Just wasn't up for company, I guess," I said, shrugging my shoulders. "I'm Bailey, by the way."

"Jackson. Jackson Gregory," he explained, offering a hand to me. I took it slowly, shaking it gently. He smiled at my shyness. "I'm surprised I've never met you before."

"Well I don't go out much," I noted again.

"I know, but I've lived here my whole life. I don't live too far away from this neighborhood."

"My older sister Lanie always took me to parties, but I haven't gone since..." I mumbled off, asking myself if it was the right thing to do to tell this perfect stranger about my deceased sister. I thought the better of it and waited for him to respond. When I raised my eyes to his, he was looking at me a face full of confusion.

"Wait a minute. What was your last name again?" he asked.

"Keys," I said slowly, trying to figure out what he was getting at.

"Holy shit," he muttered, going to take a sip of his drink. When he finished, he grinned back down at me. "I'm Brayden's cousin."

My eyes widened so big that I was almost certain they would fall out of the sockets. My breathing sped up again, knowing that this was just another connection to Lanie that I would be forced to deal with. I didn't know if I was ready to let more people in that knew about her. I wasn't ready to talk about her again.

"Lanie's...Brayden?" I questioned slowly, praying he would find himself mistaken and forfeit this conversation altogether.

"Yes!" he exclaimed, grinning like a mad man. "I can't believe this is the infamous Bailey Keys I'm speaking to!"

"What do you mean infamous?" I asked. I'd never met him in my life and I was pretty sure Lanie never mentioned Brayden's cousin named Jackson. I hadn't a clue how he knew me either.

"Lanie talked about you constantly at family parties," he went on. "It was always Bailey this and Bailey that, no matter what someone asked her about. She'd always say 'Bailey's so gorgeous,' 'Bailey's a genius,' 'She's such a sweetheart.' She always had such amazing things to say about you. Jesus, it's a wonder I hadn't met you sooner..."

"But I don't even know who you are..." I mumbled, mostly to myself. I didn't even know that she used to talk about me that much to other people, especially ones I didn't know myself. The only people on Brayden's side of the family that I met were his mother and father at a family get together once.

"I know," he said, sounding sort of sullen at the thought. "My parents were always away on business so I never got to go the engagement party...or even the wedding, because they were always out of state."

"But I didn't even see you at the funeral..." I went on.

"I wanted to go," he exclaimed, a frown creased in his features. "Bray didn't want all of those people from his side of the family bombarding your side. He said it would be too much because the family was so big. We all loved Lanie though. We wanted to..." he sighed heavily. "We wanted to be there for her."

I watched him closely, sort of smiling at the amount of care this boy possessed for my sister. It was almost like he knew her just as well as I did, and loved her all the same. If anyone would be the one to understand how I feel, it would be him.

"Wow. I can't believe all of that," I breathed, running a hand through the mess of curls Annabelle had done earlier.

"I can't believe I'm meeting you," he said, eyeing me with a look so full of admiration, I was almost speechless. "The way she talked about you...god it was like I almost knew you myself. I wanted to meet you so badly one day, to meet the real Bailey. Spend time with her, you know? But...she definitely was not lying about the gorgeous part."

I blushed a little and smiled thoughtfully at his words, boldly reaching over to him. I placed my hand on his that was resting on his thigh and he smiled wide.

"That's so nice of you," I said. "I wish I could have met you sooner."

"Me too. Do you think..." he went to ask, but my phone beeped from somewhere in the recesses of my cardigan I put on earlier. I pulled it out and smiled at the screen.

"That boy I left with was the definition of scum. I'm ready to leave, meet me by the front door. –Anna"

I wrote her a quick reply, explaining that I would be downstairs in a minute, before meeting Jackson's eyes again. He smiled big at me again, that look of admiration still clear in his features. I could feel my heart soaring at the look, just knowing at least someone appreciated me. And it was all thanks to Lanie.

"I have to go," I said, almost regretfully.

His smile dropped some. "Before you go, is there anyway we could...you know meet up sometime? I want to get to know you myself," he said, the grin returning.

His smile was contagious, I realized, when my lips curved like this. "Sure," I said, before giving him my number and telling him to text me when he thought of a good place and time to meet up again.

Before I opened the door up again that night, Jackson called me back. "It was really nice to finally meet you Bailey."

I grinned at him, almost blushing. I think I could get used to a boy like Jackson. "It was nice to finally meet you too, Jackson."

I waved my fingers at him before shutting the door behind me and making my way back downstairs. I didn't know the grin was still apparent on my face until I met Annabelle at the door and she eyed me curiously. I followed her outside of the noisy house and to her car while she questioned me.

"What's got you so happy?" she asked, smiling a little herself. "Is it a boy...?"

"Sort of..." I went on. "It's not what you think though," I explained, raising a hand to her.

"Oh bullshit," she playfully scoffed. "What's his name?"

"His name is Jackson and there's nothing going on between us. He knows me through Lanie and Brayden," I explained further.

"Seriously?" she said, stopping in her tracks. "Wow, how does he know you then?"

"He's a cousin of Brayden's and apparently Lanie talked about me at family parties a lot..." I said carelessly, with a wave of the hand.

We got into her car and she was silent for a few moments, contemplating what to say as she started the engine. "Well what did you guys talk about?"

"Lanie and me mostly. He said he's wanted to meet me for years and how he felt like he already knew me. He smiled a lot too..." I noted.

"Oh he so likes you!" she exclaimed, smacking a hand on her steering wheel as we drove off.

"He does not! We literally just met. He was just being nice to me, that's all."

"Did he call you pretty or anything? Did he compliment you at all?" she asked, making a turn down my street.

"Well he did call me gorgeous..." I mentioned, acting like it meant nothing.

"Jackson totally has a thing for you, Bails!"

"He doesn't!" I yelled back at her again. My phone beeped in my cardigan pocket and I pulled it out while she went on about the mysterious boy.

"I still can't believe I finally met you, gorgeous. Meet me at the coffee shop on sixth and Tyson Road tomorrow afternoon around 4? (: – Jackson"

I smiled at the screen and wrote a quick response.

"Of course. I'll text you when I leave tomorrow (: - Bailey"

"Why are you all smiles again?" Annabelle questioned, looking over at me as she drove.

"No reason," I shrugged, putting my phone back into my pocket.

"Was that Jackson?" she asked, smacking me when I shrugged at her again. "It was him wasn't it?"

"Yes it was him! We're just meeting for coffee tomorrow. It's no big deal!"

"No big deal? Oh Jackson's got you already and he doesn't even know it," she muttered, turning into my driveway.

I only smiled in response to her inquiries as I said goodnight and wandered up the pathway to my house. I didn't know why I was suddenly so happy about meeting a random guy at a party. Maybe it was because he knew Lanie. Or maybe it was because he was treating me like I actually mattered.

All I knew was that right now, Evan Warren was the furthest thing from my mind.

Chapter 21

Bailey Keys was seriously the only thing my brain would focus on.

It was quite ridiculous honestly. I wasn't one to dwell on girls like this, especially ones who kept bringing me down. I knew it was mostly my own fault. I was the one decided to be with Leslie, and I'd betrayed Bailey's trust in me more times than one. I just wish there was some way I could fix it all and make amends again.

I couldn't just let a girl like that go. She practically held my heart in her two small hands and she didn't even know it. Even just looking at me with that face filled disgust and eyes filled with distrust made my heart fall to the depths of my stomach and my facial features cringe at the thought. Seeing her like that at her door a few days ago made me feel sick, and I constantly kept cursing myself for even making her go through all of the things I have since the day that I met her.

It really was my entire fault.

I'd spent the majority of my days at school, since college was starting. Even though I could barely concentrate on the lectures and notes on the slides, I tried my hardest to make her leave the confinements of my mind and push school in its place. It was really the only thing I could do without making myself feel like complete and utter shit.

The times that I wasn't sitting in class and absentmindedly letting my thoughts wonder, I was at Aaron's house, eating all of his food or participating in a battle for a video game, just so I wouldn't be left alone with my mind. Aaron tried his hardest to get my mind off of the whole thing, but it was no use to me.

I didn't even know what to call our fight. I didn't know if it was a break up, or small fight that I thought we could get over and stay a couple. I couldn't even call us a couple if I wanted to, because we'd really only lasted a few days before ending it all at the foot of her doorstep. The entirety of the situation was difficult enough for me to decipher, let alone dragging my mother or Aaron into it.

My mom would sit at dinner and continue to ask me night after night why Bailey wasn't at the house, and I would always reply with a simple, 'She's busy tonight.' When that became an every night thing and my mother finally figured out that I was lying, she sat me down and asked me what really happened and I couldn't lie to her anymore. I told her everything I had done to Bailey as she sat and listened with a grim look on her face.

"Why haven't you tried to make it up her, Evan?" she cooed, placing a firm hand on the table.

She seemed quite outraged that I let a girl like Bailey slip from my fingertips, but she only mirrored how I felt about the events before me. I felt just as angry and upset as she showed.

"I tried," I sighed, placing my head in my hands. I let out something of a mix of a frustrated sigh and a heavy growl.

"You haven't tried hard enough. Do you know your father and I went through almost the same exact situation you two are having?"

I lifted my head and widened my eyes a bit. "You did?"

She simply nodded before continuing. "You see, you're definitely your father's son," she winked. "He had such a terrible time letting others in. He thought he was too tough for emotions and just carried on his life being a stubborn, hard headed man like yourself."

"Mom it's not because I'm too-" I went to say, but she cut me off with a raise of the hand.

"Let me finish," she scolded, eyeing me daringly. I silenced myself and let her continue. "Your father never wanted to tell me what was going on in his life. You know your grandmother got sick when he was a teenage boy, her breast cancer beginning to get out of control."

I nodded my head, the smiling pictures they used to show me creating a slideshow through my mind.

"I didn't know about that until well into your father and I's relationship. It took one more breakdown in his life for him to finally come out and tell me what was going on all along. I didn't talk to him for weeks after he said a few choice things about me out of anger. But then one day, he showed up at my doorstep, explaining everything to me and how sorry he was for doing such awful things. I couldn't let him go after that," she said, tearing up slightly at the memory. "All it takes sometimes is a little understanding, and the light at the end of the tunnel will soon appear," she said, her voice tight with tears.

I grabbed onto her hand that on the table and squeezed lightly. She smiled small at me and cleared her throat.

"Now go tell that girl how much you care for and why you've been such an immense jerk to her," she scolded, pointing a finger at me.

I smiled at her words before letting it slip from my lips. "I've already explained everything. It's the part where she has the picture that's tough."

"Go to her and explain everything. I'm not just talking about your father. I'm talking about your feelings for everything around you. Let her in so she can have the full view of the amazing man I've raised today."

I got up from the table and hugged my mother tightly, not letting her slip from my arms. She always seemed to know what to say to lighten anything going on in my life, and today was no different. I knew that if I couldn't count on anyone else, she would be the one that I could. I knew she was right, and I had to go see Bailey and let her see the full version of me. I couldn't limit myself to others, and I needed to really explain why I did and said the things that I have.

It was all I could do to get her back.

An hour later, I'd wondered into the coffee shop that I knew Bailey always loved to go to. I'd always pick her up her favorite, a tall caramel macchiato, and bring it to her whenever we hung out. Now that those days were few and far between, I noticed I hadn't stepped foot in this place in a while, and it was quite eerie as I smelled the strong scent of coffee hit me when I walked through the door.

I made a beeline for the long stretch of people waiting for their beverages, before my jaw almost dislocated itself from my face and my heart pounded in a familiar but now uncomfortable way.

The laugh that was almost music to my ears and the smile that made my heart race was now given to another man, sitting in front of the girl I'd meant to see in almost twenty minutes. She was here, sitting at a table near the huge display window, sipping lightly on her cup while grinning at the guy before her. His back was turned to me, so I couldn't make out who he was. I tried my best to maneuver my head in a way that I could see him, but ended up looking an idiot and catching Bailey's attention unwillingly.

The smile that once graced her lips vanished in a flash, and the guy who was laughing with her, turned his head to see where her eyes had fallen. I shifted my feet uncomfortably, not knowing what to do. At the last minute, I figured I should walk over there and say something, instead of being stared at for more uncomfortable minutes.

"Bails," I said, my voice almost sounding breathless as I took her in.

It had been days since I laid eyes on her and I wasn't quite sure what I would say. What I had planned to say at her house, alone, definitely wasn't going to cut it here with all these people in a public place. I shoved my hands in the pockets of my jeans as my mind wandered, searching for the right words to say.

"What are you doing here?" she asked, malice seeping through her tone. I almost cringed at the way it sounded.

"I was actually here to pick up your favorite. I was going to see if we could talk about..." I continued, but a sharp clearing of the throat came from the other side of me, the side I'd clearly been ignoring.

I turned to face him, almost clenching my fists at the sight of him. It took all of it in me not to jump over the table and beat the smirk right off his boy band looking face.

"Jackson," I growled, my arms crossing over my chest.

He grinned victoriously at me. "Evan."

"How do you guys know each other?" Bailey asked cautiously, eyes darting in between the both of us.

"Oh Evan and I go way back," he started, still keeping his eyes firmly trained on mine. It was like he knew I was ready to pounce and he was waiting to retaliate.

"Always find some way into my life, don't you Gregory?"

"Not my fault that they always come to..." He went to say, but Bailey cut him off by pulling me by the arm and dragging me out the front door.

"I'll be right back," she quickly said toJackson, earning another victorious smile from him to me.

When we got outside, she pushed me against the side of the brick building. I didn't even wince at the contact, my mind still whirling with the fact that Jackson Gregory was back in my territory, stealing the very things that I wanted.

He always found some way to get to me.

"What the hell are you doing here, huh? How many times do I have to tell you that I don't trust you anymore! I can't be around someone who..."

I cut her off, my brain finally trained on the beautiful girl before me. "Someone who you can't trust? I'm someone you can't trust?! How about the asshole sitting at the table with you is someone you can't trust!"

"What are you on about, Warren?" she asked, her voice still dripping with anger as she said my name.

"Jackson's the biggest asshole you could come in contact with, Bails! He's played every girl he's been with. He's taken everything from me! Ever since we were kids he's done nothing but barge into my territory and takes the things I've wanted or had."

"Let's get something straight here," she butted in. "I'm not yours anymore! At this point, I don't even think I was yours to begin with. Jackson's nice to me. He cares about what I have to say. He listens when I speak to him. And he sure as hell doesn't keep things from me!"

"But he lies, Bailey! Don't you see that?" I exclaimed, throwing my hands in the air in massive frustration.

"No he doesn't! Who are you judge people on the truth when you've done nothing but lie to me and keep things from me?" she shouted, pushing me against the wall again.

By now, her cheeks were flamed with red, mimicking her anger through her cheekbones. I let her push me time and time again, letting her get the frustration out.

When she calmed down and took a few steps back, I continued. "Now I told you, I may have kept so many things from you, Bailey. But I never once lied to you!"

"How am I supposed to believe that?!" she quipped.

My heart was still racing uncomfortably in my chest as I watched the event unfold before me. I knew at this point thatJacksonwas going to get my girl. I couldn't stop her from seeing him, no matter how hard I beat the shit out of him as a warning. I couldn't hold her back from what she wanted to do. At the least bit, I could let her be happy. But I just couldn't let her be happy with someone like Jackson who I knew was going to hurt her.

Ever since we were young, Jackson Gregory always found a way to take the things I wanted. He took the toys from my hands as a pre-schooler, and the girls from my arms as a teenager. There wasn't ever a thing in life thatJacksoncouldn't take if he wanted it. And I knew at this point, that I couldn't stop Bailey from going after the things she wanted.

No matter how much I told her that she would be hurt in the end.

"I'm so unbelievably sorry, baby. You have to believe me. The things I've kept from you and the things I've said can't be taken back and I know that. But I can't stand to see you hurt again!"

I frowned as her eyes seemed to capture every emotion she was feeling in one fleeting moment; anger, sadness, betrayal, hurt...and what I almost thought was love. I could only hope for that.

"You know I have no reason to trust you," she said, her voice thickened with tears. I knew she was trying hard to hold them back, but a few traitors had made their way past her lashes to her cheeks. It took all of it in me not to walk up to her and brush them away.

"I know that," I sighed heavily. "Please, give me the chance to make it up to you and show you how much you mean to me, baby. Please..."

I was begging at this point, I knew that. It would be sheer and utter humiliation if anyone I knew saw the wreck I was at this moment, but I didn't care. If pleading gave me a chance, I'd be on my hands and knees if she asked.

"I'm not your baby," she sighed, closing her eyes tightly for a few furious moments. When she opened them, they were hard with determination. It was almost too hard to figure out what she was so determined to do. "And, so help me God, I will get over you Evan Warren."

"Bailey," I breathed.

She shook her head, her red tendrils bouncing back and forth against her cheeks. "No, Evan. I'm tired of hurting! Can't you see that?" she wailed.

"I don't mean to hurt you..." I murmured, reaching out to wipe the second round of tears.

She pushed my arm away furiously, eyeing me with a hard gaze. "IfJacksonis someone I can get over you with, then I'll make it happen. I'm done hurting all of the time, Evan. I thought you'd be the one to take it all away, erase the pain I had left. But you're the cause of it now! I can't keep fighting with you and crying all of the time like this! I need you to stay the hell out of my life from now on, okay? I'm done," she yelled the last part, eyeing me almost regretfully one last time before walking back into the coffee shop, joining my brand new replacement.

I fell against the wall, sliding onto my butt and sticking my head in my hands. I gripped the ends of my hair roughly, filled with so much frustration and sadness it was almost hard to bare at this point. There was absolutely nothing left to do to win her back. I'd lost the one person who I could finally open up to and be myself with. I finally found someone who understood what the empty space in your heart left by a passed on loved one was like. But she was gone for good.

And I didn't know how I felt about that new permanent empty space.

Epilogue

G iving up on Evan wasn't something I wanted to do; it was something that I needed to do.

Evan had been my rock to a certain point, and was once someone I could see actually taking all of the pain away. But his one, but serious, flaw was that he continued to hurt me in some way or another. I'd tried my hardest to give him the chances he thought he deserved, and the chance for my heart to heal, just like Lanie told me too. But after receiving the picture from Leslie and the numerous stabs at the heart on my end, I just couldn't put up with the misery anymore.

There came a time in anyone's life when they had the choice between doing what they wanted and doing what they thought was right. I wasn't fond of my decision in the end. I walked away from that conversation with my nails permanently implanted into the palms of my skin and my face soaked in my own tears. My heart didn't want it, but my mind knew it was what was right. There was room for someone else in my life now, and I was finding myself crossing my fingers that he wouldn't be the one to crush my heart all over again.

I'd spent two whole months getting to know Jackson before I even let him kiss me on the lips after a date. He let me in so easily, unlike a certain firefighter's son had. He made me laugh and smile in the moments I found myself needing it the most. Jackson's arms suddenly felt like a place I was meant to fit in. It was a safe haven of sorts, a place I could fall to when I needed to be caught.

What made matters even better when having a boyfriend like Jackson was that he knew the girl that Lanie was. It was almost effortless when I spoke to him about her; my feelings, my tears, my smiles, all suddenly became as easy to talk about as breathing had come to me. He understood the sadness I felt when it came to her loss and knew some of the funny things about my lost sister that he laughed along with. I almost found myself wondering what took me so long to find a boy like him, and even more why I wasted my time on a boy who did nothing but hurt me.

I wasn't saying that I was promptly over Evan; I was quite far from it. No matter how much Jackson etched his way into my heart, I still found that the hole Jackson was meant to fill was still empty. Jackson was digging his own burrow, and Evan's seemed to be forever left empty. I didn't know what it was about him, that he was forever stuck in the confinements of my heart and mind.

But I did know that I was going to try my hardest to let Jackson be the only one my heart was stuck on.

As I walked the pathway up to Jackson's house, I folded my arms across my chest, bringing the jacket closer against my body. The late November weather was making its way to the neighborhood soon, and I was relishing in the fact that I was going to able to spend holidays without the sadness of missing Lanie at the dinner table. I'd have someone to calm me down, someone to grab my hand and squeeze, releasing the pressure from the sadness with a simple gesture. I was getting quite used to the idea of having someone to rely on from now on.

Jackson and I had made plans a few days earlier in the week to help my parents pick up a few favors for the Thanksgiving dinner they were holding for our big family in a week. He told me that he'd be happy to help, and our relationship was becoming so comfortable that I found myself just letting myself through the door. He lived alone, being the simple age of 21 and going to the college around the corner.

I smiled as I turned the knob, knowing I'd be in the comforting arms of my boyfriend's in a few moments. I walked to the kitchen, where I usually found him stuffing his face when I let myself in. I frowned a little when he was nowhere to be found in the first level of the house. I was about to call his name, my mouth getting ready to move, when I heard a gut-wrenching noise that shouldn't be heard from a girlfriend.

The strenuous noise of a moan of sorts made its way down the stairs to my unwilling ears, freezing me to a halt at the bottom stair. I wasn't quite sure whether or not I wanted to go upstairs. My mind was trying hard to prepare me for the blow I figured I would be receiving when I opened the door to his room, but my heart was trying to convince me that it could just be the unflattering sound of his parents. Jackson couldn't even be home for all I knew.

I swallowed hard and squeezed my eyes shut as I prepared to move my feet mechanically up the stairs. I cringed when I heard a shrill moaning sound again, weirdly hoping I was wrong and Jackson wasn't even home. As I heard the noise again, quicker in succession this time, I found myself walking quicker up the stairs and froze again at the bedroom door that it was coming from. My heart pounded uncomfortably in my chest, grasping the familiarity of my boyfriend's bedroom door.

With one last hope hanging by a string, praying it wasn't him, I turned the knob slowly as the door creaked open. I felt my heart shred to pieces, making confetti pieces at the bottom of my stomach. I almost threw up at the sight, taking in my boyfriend on the bed with an all too familiar blonde sitting on top of him. They were both clearly naked and engaging in something that should have been me and him.

Something must have hit them because Jackson turned his head towards the doorway I was frozen in and squeezed the blonde's hips tightly to get her attention. She looked down at him, confused, but followed his eye line to me, my limbs stuck to a standstill. I couldn't find any words, or any rational movements to get myself out of the situation. I wanted to run, but my feet didn't seem to get the message. I wanted to scream, but my lips remained tight.

The one thing I didn't want to do in front of them was cry, but my eyes decided they were going to be the only part of my body to listen to me that day.

Silent tears made their way down my cheeks as I watched Jackson cringe.

"Baby, it's not what it looks like!" he said hurriedly, pushing the blonde off to the side and covering his nether regions with a simple white sheet.

He came over to me and waved his hands around anxiously. I wasn't hearing a word he was saying, deciding that they were most likely a bag full of lies to try to get me to "understand." I couldn't seem to get my eyes off of the blonde who was smirking victoriously while she found her panties. She was bathed in pride almost, flicking her blonde locks over her shoulder as she took me in. She held back a giggle with the flick of a hand as she watched me cry in front of her.

It was almost like she knew that she won and she was glorifying it.

"Bails! Please, say something," he breathed, panting after the rant I seemed to block out.

I finally decided to avert my watery eyes over to his widened and worried ones, and I frowned at him. He frowned back, knowing what was coming.

"How...how could...you?" I panted, my heart feeling like it was running a marathon.

"I didn't mean for this to happen!" he screamed, running over to the other side of his room to put on a pair of jeans crumpled on the floor.

"For what to happen? For me to find out?!" I screamed, throwing my hands up in the air.

The blonde sauntered over to Jackson, laying her hands on his shoulders and sitting her chin against him. She was rubbing her riches in my face, the smirk still firmly planted on her lips. If I wasn't so upset and confused, I would have been ready to hop over the idiot in front of me and rip the blonde locks from her pretty little head.

The odd thing was that Jackson didn't make a move to remove her from his shoulder. He didn't shrug her off, or scold her for doing such terrible things in front of his girlfriend. He just let her faun over him, like they were both in on something I knew nothing about.

"Poor Bailey," Leslie sarcastically pouted. "It must suck to find out like this."

"Find out what..." I questioned, keeping my eyes firm on Jackson's.

"This has been going on for a long time," she went on, talking to me like I was a child who needed to be told twice. "Almost as long as you guys have been...what did you guys call it? Oh, dating."

"I thought you...I thought," I went to say, but found my breathing blocking any coherent form of speech.

"He clearly wasn't getting anything from you. So he came to me," she squeaked, smiling again, victoriously, while rubbing the back of Jackson's hair affectionately.

"First the picture..." I breathed. "And now this."

She laughed maniacally. "That picture was just to get back at you, idiot. It was from when we were together. I just wanted you to taste a little bit of the medicine you gave me when you stole Evan from me."

"But..." I panted again.

"God, you really are an idiot. Bailey just can't seem to keep the men in her life can she..." she smirked, placing a kiss upon Jackson's shoulder.

I took the sight in again, almost in the need of a pinch, hoping the amount of bullshit before me was all a dream. Jackson couldn't have been this cruel to me. I expected this much from a girl like Leslie, but not him. I finally let him in, and he paid me back by sleeping with someone behind my back to entire time.

The part I believe that hurt more was watching him in front of me, letting Leslie touch him and grope him like he was her prize. He wasn't even putting on a show to convince me that nothing was going on. He was letting Leslie do the talking, like he didn't even give a shit what I thought of this whole mess.

"Bailey," he finally croaked out, reaching out a hand to me.

I snapped it back almost instantly. "No! No! You don't get to act all hurt and guilty when you're just standing there, letting her talk to me like that! I can't believe you would do this to me!" I yelled out.

Before he could even respond, I ran down the stairs and out the door. Tears were freely falling now, as I wasn't even making an attempt to get rid of them. I ran down the street and slowed to a fast walk as I ran through what had just happened. I was in utter shock that this was happening to me. They had been doing things behind my back the entire time and I hadn't a clue. I felt disgusted, stupid and overall finished with everyone in my life.

I didn't find the point in finding others to comfort my pain. I was realizing that I conquered my own pain, and I shouldn't be relying on others to hide it. I was in a mess of internal pain, and no one was going to fix that other than myself. But, the more I kept telling myself that I was the conqueror of my own pain, the more I found myself needing a pair of arms to lie in while I wept everything out. I was emotionally drained from energy and I need to let it all out for once in my entire life.

I called the one person who held that familiar comfort. I didn't know if they would answer. I didn't even know if they cared enough anymore to hold me and tell me that things were going to be okay again if they had any say in it.

When they answered the door, I fell right into their arms. I let it all out, crying into the familiar shirt and recognizing the smell I knew that I missed. I cried for what felt like hours, my chest heaving and arms shaking. I cried out for Lanie, I cried out for the absence of my parents, for losing Evan, for losing Jackson and even for Leslie. I couldn't shake the image of the two on the bed and Jackson's behavior when it unfolded before me.

I just let the person I knew would help lead me upstairs to their room and hold me until I finished. Not once did they silence me, or try to stop me from crying out. They just squeezed me until I felt I could pop and waited for me to finish.

I awoke the next morning with a familiar pair of arms around me and a smiling face looking upon me. I felt myself smiling small back at him.

"You okay now?" Evan asked, rubbing circles against my arm with his rough fingers.

I took in a heavy needed breath and shook my head. "No," I simply said.

I wrapped my arms around his torso, relishing in his familiar scent and favorite shirt. He took a few minutes, probably figuring out what to say that seemed right, before he sat up against his headboard, bring me along with him. I still kept my arms hooked around his torso, needing the comfort a little too much.

"I think you'll be okay, you know," he said, smoothing my hair against my head and placing a kiss in the spot.

"And how do you know that?" I questioned, looking up at him beneath my lashes.

"Because you're the strongest girl I know. You can get through anything, Bails."

I sighed heavily, unhooking my arms from his. I was almost disgusted with myself that I treated him the way that I did and he was taking me in again. It was effortless for him to take me back in his arms and feed me lines from his heart. I felt bad for even questioning his actions in the first place.

"How can you sit there and hold me, tell me things will be okay and say things like...well that," I went on, pointing a finger at him. "When I've been nothing but terrible to you?"

He huffed before pushing up his body with his hands. He took his hands in mine, stroking the knuckles soothingly before getting ready to speak. I found that I couldn't even take my eyes off of his when he began.

"We've been through nothing but shit, for what seems to be our whole lives. Granted, our only similarity is that we've known the pain of losing a loved one. But, you understand how I feel more than any other person in my life. You're like my light at the end of this stupid tunnel I call my life. No matter the fucking pain I'm writhing in or the sadness I'm dwelling in, you're always there. Sometimes, you're even there unknowingly. You can just wrap your arms around me or smile at me and I'm suddenly forgetting everything I'm so pissed off or upset about."

"But," I went to cut in, but he shushed me with a push of his finger against my lips.

"Sh, I'm not finished. I did some pretty bad things to you, too. As much as you're there for me, I wasn't there for you when you needed someone to hang onto. I wanted so much to be the guy you fall back on when you've had a bad day, or the first one you come to when you're having a good day and need to brag about it. I wanted to be the guy you called in the middle of the night when you're upset or had a bad dream. But most of all, I wanted to be the guy who understood you the most, just like how I feel about you. God, you're my everything and you don't even know it half the time," he laughed softly, shaking his head.

"Evan," I breathed, placing my hand against his stubbly cheek.

I was just now taking in his new features, noticing the contrasts from two months ago. His face was lacking in shaving, the stubbles scratching against my palm as I rubbed his cheek gently with my fingers. His eyes seemed more sunken in then before, most likely from lack of sleep. And for the first time since I'd known him, his hair wasn't styled and primped, but more laid back and like he'd just woken up.

"Bails, I want to be with you and only you, one hundred percent. I'm so sorry for how I've treated you in the past. I want to share everything with you, give you my all. I'm tired of hiding behind this fucking brick wall I always put up. If it means you'll the do the same with me, I'm ready to give you all of me. If you'll take it of course..." he smiled sheepishly.

My heart was pounding in my chest, but this time it was a comfortable sensation, one that I'd come to have felt whenever I was around Evan. I was almost choked up at the thought of him giving me his all. He wanted that badly to be with me that he was willing to break down the barriers he'd taken almost ten years to build. I didn't even believe I deserved that much.

But he did.

"Of course I'll have you," I breathed, a smile gracing my lips. I leant in almost instantly, meeting him the bliss of the middle for a kiss.

He'd placed his hand on my cheek, mimicking my movements, as he kissed me back. It was filled with so much passion, I felt like I would burst at the contact. He ran his tongue across my lips, asking for entrance, and I granted it quickly. I pulled at the ends of his hair as I slid on his lap. He wrapped his hands around my waist, bringing me as close at the proximity would allow. As we kissed, I felt my heart swell. I brought in his warmth, his tenderness when he kissed me, the rough feel of his hands as they played at the ends of my shirt. Every nerve ending was on fire with each touch, for once signaling that it was okay to be this way with someone.

Evan was the boy I could trust at the end of the day. He had made mistakes, ones I myself could always understand. He'd broken down his walls to let a girl like me in, just because he loved and trusted me enough to do so. He wasn't going to cheat on me; no matter how many times my mind would try to convince me otherwise. He wasn't to going to block my feelings like they didn't mean anything to him. Evan would be the only one who understood the power of a broken heart, and the flaws that come with it.

As we relished in the new found love we were promising to carry on, I found myself silently thanking Mr. Warren and Lanie. Without Mr. Warren, Evan wouldn't be here. He wouldn't be the man he is today if Gregory hadn't instilled such grace in his son. Evan wouldn't be the powerful, yet broken man who I knew today without the loss and the strength that came with it.

Without Lanie, I wouldn't have had the heart to take the leap I'd needed all along. Lanie had always been my rock, ever since we were young. She had been the one person who wouldn't let me down in life until she left me on that fateful day. Without her push in the letter she left and the strength she unknowingly had instilled in me since day one, I wouldn't be here, in Evan's arms, finally knowing what it was like to give your all for the one you loved.

When it came down to it, wounded hearts really had the power to conquer all. Even alone, you can be strong enough to overcome any obstacle in your way. Otherwise, life would be filled with boring, day to day events that didn't end up surprising you in the end. You could surprise yourself one day, with how much courage your broken heart can hold.

Wounded hearts really do have the power to conquer.